CORFIOT TALES

J. M. Q. DAVIES attended Greek schools during his childhood in Thessaloniki and read Modern Greek and German at Oxford before pursuing an academic career in English and Comparative Literature, teaching at the Universities of California, Alberta, Melbourne, Darwin and Waseda. He is the author of a monograph, *Blake's Milton designs: the dynamics of meaning* (1993), has edited a collection of essays, *Bridging the gap: literary theory in the classroom* (1994), and written articles on modern fiction, literary theory, fantasy and new literatures in English. His translations from German and Modern Greek are:

German tales of fantasy, horror and the grotesque (Longman Cheshire, 1987)

ARTHUR SCHNITZLER, *Selected short fiction* (Angel Classics, 1999) — *Dream story* (Penguin, 1999) — *Round dance and other plays* (Oxford World's Classics, 2004)

THOMAS SCHIPPERGES, *Prokofiev* (Haus, 2003)

HUGO VON HOFMANNSTHAL, *Selected tales* (Angel Classics, 2007)

KONSTANTINOS THEOTOKIS, *Slaves in their chains* (Angel Classics, 2014) *The life and death of Hangman Thomas* (Colenso Books, 2016)

OTHER TRANSLATIONS OF GREEK LITERATURE
FROM COLENSO BOOKS

Sweet-voiced Sappho, verse translations from SAPPHO and other Ancient Greek poets by Theodore Stephanides (2015)

IAKOVOS KAMBANELLIS, *Three plays (The courtyard of wonders, The four legs of the table, Ibsenland)* translated by Marjorie Chambers (2015)

KONSTANTINOS THEOTOKIS, *The life and death of Hangman Thomas* translated by J. M. Q. Davies (2016)

Five hundred epigrams from the Greek Anthology translated by Theodore Stephanides (expected 2018)

CORFIOT TALES

by

KONSTANTINOS THEOTOKIS

*translated from the Greek
with an Introduction and Notes*

by

J. M. Q. DAVIES

COLENSO BOOKS
2017

This translation first published October 2017 by
Colenso Books
68 Palatine Road, London N16 8ST, UK
colensobooks@gmail.com

Reprinted with minor corrections December 2017

ISBN 978-0-9928632-5-8

Translation, Introduction and Notes copyright © 2017 J. M. Q. Davies

These stories, except for 'Illicit love', were first published
as a collection in 1935 by Ἑταιρεία πρὸς Ἐνίσχυσιν
τῶν Ἑπτανησιακῶν Μελέτων, Corfu,
as *Κορφιάτικες Ἱστορίες*, edited by Eirini Dendrinou.
'Ilicit love', was first published in 1977 by Καστανιώτης, Athens,
as *Ἀγάπη παράνομη: διήγημα ἀνέκδοτο*, edited by Philippos Vlachos.

The image of a Greek village dance on the front cover
is from a painting by Valias Semertzidis (1911–1983).
The portrait of Theotokis on the back cover
is by Aglaïa Pappa (1903–1984).
We have been unable to establish the location or ownership of,
or copyright interest in, either of the paintings.
We will gladly add acknowledgements to subsequent
printings if the information is provided.

Printed and bound in Great Britain by
Lightning Source UK Ltd
Chapter House, Pitfield, Kiln Farm
Milton Keynes MK11 3LW, UK

CONTENTS

Introduction	vii
Face down	1
Not done yet?	3
Cain	7
Village life	17
Reputation	29
Honourable people	45
Stalakti's wedding	51
Illicit love	69
Two loves	109
Was it a sin?	143
Notes	148
Bibliography	155

INTRODUCTION

Increasingly included on the Grand Tour by late eighteenth century travellers, Corfu and the Ionian Islands, with their picturesque Homeric landscapes, ruined forts and dual Greek–Italian names, are culturally distinct from the other isles of Greece. Hugging the eastern Adriatic coast from mountainous Albania to the tip of Crete, they lie on the fault-line between old Rome and Byzantium, between Catholic west and Orthodox and Islamic east, between Cross and Crescent. And by the time of the sacking of Constantinople by the Fourth Crusade en route to Jerusalem in 1204, which hastened the break-up of the Byzantine empire, they were being fought over as military strongholds and trading entrepôts by Genoese, Angevins, Normans and Venetians. In 1386 Corfu, the most northerly and fertile of them, was purchased by the Venetians, who, after the fall of Constantinople to the Turks in 1453, massively extended the island's fortifications, holding out against two protracted Turkish sieges in 1537 and 1716. And once Crete — the jewel in Venice's maritime crown — succumbed in 1667, Corfu remained the only significant Greek island never to come under Ottoman dominion, providing a vital cultural link between east and west and a beacon of hope for Greek nationalist and irredentist aspirations.

Landless itself, the Venetian Republic ran Corfu and Zante much like Crete as food-producing colonies, establishing a quasi-feudal Greco–Italian landed aristocracy (their names entered into a local honour role, or *Libro d' Oro*), paying a bounty for every thousand olive trees planted, and monopolizing the export trade in currants, oil and salt. And though nominally Catholic, the Venetians took a pragmatic approach to religion, allowing an Orthodox *Protopapas*, appointed by the Patriarchate in Constantinople, to coexist alongside the ranking Catholic archbishop, the two together processing the relics of the island's patron, St Spyridon, around the town on festive occasions. Jewish refugees from the Spanish Inquisition also found safe haven in Corfu (where the ghetto was locked up at night), some prospering in finance, others employed in the galleys or as porters. But the cost of defending the islands meant that Venice neglected public education, and higher legal and medical training had to be obtained abroad, commonly in Padua. And as life in town became more agreeable, absentee landlordism increased, the nobles forsaking their Italianate country houses, or *archondika*, and exploiting their peasants to pay for opera seats and gambling, and the peasants held back by archaic farming methods, irregular harvests, debt, disease, ill-educated priests and age-old superstitions.

During the Napoleonic Wars the Ionian Islands again found themselves in the vortex of international affairs due to their strategic location — Napoleon, after taking Venice in 1797 and with his eye on Egypt, famously called them the 'key to the Adriatic' and 'worth all of Italy' — and Corfu was occupied in quick succession by all the major Powers. In line with their republican convictions, the French burned the *Libro d'Oro* and raised Trees of Liberty, upset the clergy with their atheism and demands for educational reform, and proposed that Italian be replaced by Greek as the language of officialdom. After the Battle of the Nile, the French were supplanted by a coalition of the Russians and the Turks (traditional rivals in the Balkans) who proclaimed Corfu the capital of a semi-independent Heptanisian Republic under the protection of the Tsar. The French returned in 1807 but at the Congress of Vienna (1814–15), after Napoleon's defeat, the Ionian Islands became a British Protectorate under a series of colourful High Commissioners, assisted by a Senate drawn from the Italianate nobility, an Assembly and a Constitution.

On the Ottoman-held mainland revolutionary storm-clouds had long been gathering, Greek resentments fanned by the *Philiki Etairia*, a Christian secret society founded in Odessa. And in 1821, with the Porte distracted by a punitive war against the rogue Albanian Ali Pasha of Ioannina, the banner of Greek rebellion was raised in the Peloponnese, Theodore Kolokotronis, one of the leading warlords, crossing from Zante to take part in what would become a protracted internecine ethnic struggle. The British were bound to strict neutrality by their treaty obligations to the Turks, and firm measures were taken by the High Commissioners against Ionian radicals, or *Rizospastai*, who throughout the Protectorate continued to agitate for union with the mainland. But the Greek nationalist cause was championed by philhellenes from across Europe, notably Lord Byron, who helped raise loans in London, crossing from Cephalonia in 1823 only to succumb to

INTRODUCTION

fever outside Missolonghi. The romantic enthusiasm of the times was captured by the Zante-born Corfiot poet Count Dionysios Solomos (hailed by Goethe as the 'Byron of the east') in his ballad-like demotic 'Hymn to Liberty', verses from which became 'a second Marseillaise' and Greece's national anthem.[1]

Though disliked for their arrogance, exclusiveness and insensitivity to local customs, the British transformed Corfu almost as much during their fifty years of rule as the Venetians did in four hundred. Sir Thomas Maitland, the first High Commissioner, nicknamed 'King Tom' for his autocratic ways, created an order of St Michael and St George to immunize the title-hungry nobles against Russian interference, and introduced legal reforms that stemmed corruption and the exploitation of the peasants. An ambitious programme of public works — roads, schools, bridges, palaces and prisons — was set in train, stimulating the post-war economy, reducing the isolation of the villages and giving a Regency face to the old Venetian town, with an arcade, monuments and statues opposite the citadel and cricket on the parade-ground. In 1824 the Ionian Academy, the first modern Greek institute of higher learning, was founded by Lord Guilford, an eccentric philhellene given, as Napier put it, to 'going about dressed up like Plato with a gold band about his mad pate and flowing drapery of purple hue'[2] — an image emblematic of the misapprehension then common among the classically educated that neither the Greeks nor their language had changed since Homeric times.

After defeating the Turkish navy at the Battle of Navarino in 1827, the Powers brokered a peace between the warring factions on the mainland, and a Corfiot, Count Ioannis Kapodistrias (a seasoned diplomat in the service of the Tsar), became President of a new Greek state. After his assassination in 1831, Otto, a Bavarian, was installed as king in Athens. Northern Greece, Crete, Cyprus, Smyrna and most of the Aegean islands continued in Ottoman hands however, and Greek politics became obsessed — until after the First World War — with the *Megali Idea*, the irredentist 'great idea' of liberating and reuniting all Greeks within a new Byzantium. In 1864, following a review by Gladstone, who addressed the puzzled locals in ancient Greek, the

---

[1] Jenkins, *Dionysius Solomós*, 68.
[2] Dicks, *Corfu*, 104

British ceded all the Ionian Islands to Greece, as the price for securing their candidate, the Danish-born King George I, as Otto's successor on the throne. They departed Corfu with due military pomp, the garrison marching out of the citadel in full regalia, blowing up part of the town's fortifications as they left.

The year before, Edward Lear had published his picturesque *Views of the seven Ionian Islands*, signalling their transition from military assets to accessible wintering resorts, as steamships altered Europe's geopolitics. By the turn of the century the Greek royals had taken over Maitland's Palace of St Michael and St George and the Kaiser had purchased the tragic Habsburg Empress Elizabeth's sea-view Achilleon Palace after her assassination, adding a jetty for his yachts and motorcars. Artists like Sophie Atkinson were sketching the peasants and discovering Corfu's glorious flora on their bicycles, and archaeologists like Heinrich Schliemann, 'lured by the siren voices of Homeric geography', were exploring Cephalonia, Ithaca and Lefkada.[3] In the scramble for Ottoman territory during the First World War, Corfu briefly became a refugee camp for the Serbian army fleeing Bulgarian troops across the Albanian mountains. Italian claims to the Ionian Islands resurfaced in the 1920s and Corfu Town was heavily bombed by the Luftwaffe in 1943.

Konstantinos Theotokis, next to Solomos the Ionian Islands' most distinguished writer and one of Greece's more intriguing men of letters, was heir to these complex intellectual and cultural traditions by virtue of his birth. An idealistic Corfiot nobleman turned socialist who like Tolstoy would renounce his patrimony, he matured artistically on the very cusp of Modernism, and working principally in the *Verismo*, or Naturalist mode of Giovanni Verga (1840–1922) and Emile Zola (1840–1902), paid tribute to the harsh unrecorded lives of the Greek peasantry in terse insightful stories and novellas of immense dramatic power. And in his crowning achievement, *Slaves in their Chains* (1922), a panoramic tragicomedy and the first full-scale social novel in demotic Greek, he used his insider's knowledge to portray the old Corfiot feudal order in crisis, unequal to the struggle against the ruthlessly materialistic

---

[3] Young, *Corfu and the other Ionian Islands*, 94 provides a good summary of the archaeological quest for Homeric sites in the region.

rising middle classes.

He was the scion of one branch of the ancient Theotokis family originally from Constantinople (or Theotokoupolis, the 'city of the Mother of God'[4]), which had fled the Turks to Crete and then Corfu and been ennobled for service to the Venetian state during the seventeenth century, producing merchant buccaneers, theologians and politicians, including the first president of the Ionian Senate under the British. His father, Count Markos Theotokis, already in his forties when his elder brother Alexandros failed to produce an heir, had married the beautiful, musical seventeen-year-old Angeliki, niece of Iakovos Polylas (editor of Solomos and translator of Homer into modern Greek), and sired ten children. An early graduate of the Ionian Academy, he was much given to regaling his offspring with tales of the family's former glories, abominating the French Revolution as the work of Jews and Masons. Konstantinos, or Dinos as his eldest son was affectionately known, had a difficult nature, wilful, hot-tempered, hyperactive and prone to sleeplessness, but precociously gifted and ambitious. Brought up speaking both Italian and Greek at home and tutored privately in German, by his early teens he was already editing a news leaflet, translating Goldoni (assisted by his mother) and producing comic playlets with his siblings. At school he showed a special aptitude for maths and science, collecting insects, charting the night skies from the rooftop and even submitting papers to French professional journals.

As a student in Paris however he fell in with the city's *jeunesse dorée* — flaunting his titled status, neglecting his studies, running up huge debts which his doting uncle Alexandros secretly mortgaged the estate to repay — and after only a year left for Venice to escape a flu epidemic, without taking his degree. There, still only nineteen, he fell in love with and proposed to Ernestine von Malowitz, an (at the time impecunious) German-speaking baroness from an august Catholic Bohemian family and almost as old as his own mother — who took against her from the start. Count Markos also warned her of his son's difficult temperament and modest expectations, but she held her young suitor honour bound and on his reaching his majority the couple were married in Prague and after honeymooning in Venice moved into the family's rambling *archondiko* at Karousades in the north of Corfu,

---

[4] See Herrin, *Byzantium*, 15.

opposite Albania.

Here over the next two decades, with his well-read wife's encouragement and only occasional periods of study in Germany and Austria, Theotokis undertook an ambitious programme of self-education, immersing himself in European philosophy and literature, particularly Nietzsche, Schopenhauer and later Marx, translating extensively from Aristophanes, Lucretius, Shakespeare, Goethe, Heine, Flaubert, Turgenev and Bertrand Russell, and experimenting with fiction in both symbolist and realist modes — in the process transforming himself from budding scientist and Parisian dandy into the literary 'hermit of Karousades', as he was known to his contemporaries. His earliest experiments in fiction included *Vie de Montagne* (1895), a Greek bandit novel written in French and published with assistance from Ernestine's aunt; a prophetic rhapsody modelled on Nietzsche's *Zarathustra* entitled *Passion* (1899); and short allegorical tales influenced by Aestheticism like 'Satni's dream' and the apocalyptic 'Waning of the world'. Important to him at this stage was his friendship with the older Corfiot poet, German-trained scholar and ardent nationalist Lorentzos Mavilis (1860–1912), who bolstered his sense of identity as Greek, encouraged him to write in Greek and kindled his interest in Sanskrit. Though they would subsequently disagree politically, when insurrections broke out against the Turks in Crete (1896) and Thessaly (1897) they both took part, raising volunteer militias, and Mavilis would later meet his end on the field of battle in the First Balkan War (1912).

In 1900 Theotokis' little daughter Tina, the apple of his eye, died of meningitis, ending the idyllic phase of the marriage, Ernestine increasingly seeking consolation in her Catholic faith, he in work and occasional peccadilloes with the peasant maidens, who in those days, according to his brother Spyros, still considered pleasuring the squire a duty.[5] Typically he worked on scholarly and creative projects simultaneously, producing, for instance, an introduction to Indian literature and comparative mythology for a translation of *Shakuntala*, while also submitting his Corfiot tales to the demotic periodical *Noumas*, founded in 1903. Such regional stories, pioneered by writers like Alexandros Papadiamandis (1851–1911) and Andreas Karkavitsas (1866–1922),

---

[5] S. Theotokis, *The early years of Konstantinos Theotokis*, 69.

INTRODUCTION

were very much in vogue and dominated Greek fiction before the development of the urban social novel in the 1920s. They were categorized as *ithographia* or 'folkloric realism', and like the contemporary interest in folksong, constituted part of a drive to define Greece's post-Ottoman cultural identity.

In 1907–08 during two semesters at the university in Munich, a city already rife with revolutionary plotting, Theotokis became more seriously interested in Marxism as an alternative to Mavilis' romantic brand of nationalism. And on his return to Corfu, where small-scale industry had developed early, he joined an idealistic group of his compatriots in setting up a local socialist club, without however getting involved in day-to-day politics. His responsiveness to these trends is reflected in the centrality of class conflict in his first realistic novella, *Honour and cash* (1912), a proto-feminist work set in Corfu's harbour suburb of Mandouki, a community portrayed as still very much governed by traditional village mores. The plot focuses on a factory worker's defiance of her daughter's seducer, a debt-ridden young nobleman turned smuggler who makes exorbitant dowry demands, and is resolved (a shade tendentiously) when the daughter decides to join the workforce and bring up her child alone. His next novella in order of publication, *The Convict* (1919), is a more inward Dostoyevskian work, which raises existential questions about good and evil, injustice and self-sacrifice.[6] The protagonist, a village 'innocent' and the pariah offspring of a Turk and a Christian Albanian whore, is wrongly convicted of murdering his master, framed by the lover of his master's wife. When years later the lover (and now husband) confesses to the crime, the hero insists on his own guilt to protect the unsuspecting wife, whom he has all along idealized, and resolves to continue his sentence and minister to his fellow prisoners.

During the First World War, Theotokis' distrust of German imperialism caused him to side with the pro-Entente position of prime minister Eleftherios Venizelos in the national schism and against King Constantine, who was married to the Kaiser's sister and favoured Greek neutrality. Earlier he had refused point blank to gratify the Kaiser's request for stage adaptations of his Corfiot stories. After the

---

[6] Theotokis' last three novels were all published within four years of his death, but their order of composition overlapped and it has been suggested that *The convict* may contain his most considered reflections upon life.

war, when Ernestine was not prepared to swear allegiance to the new Czech state and forfeited her inheritance, Theotokis was obliged for the first time in his life to seek gainful employment as a civil servant in Athens.

His last two novels are both savage social satires rich in symbolism which, conspicuously in keeping with Verga's principle of *prosa dialogata*, present events dramatically through highly charged scenes and spicy idiomatic dialogue. *The life and death of Hangman Thomas* (1920) is at once a dark tragicomedy with moments of Goldonian farce, an exposé of rural squalor, disease and superstition, and a parable of capitalist exploitation. It centres on a lustful irascible old peasant nicknamed the 'hangman', who is seduced by the flirtatious village *femme fatale* next door and her avaricious brother-in-law into parting with his property in the hope of sexual favours. *Slaves in their chains* (1922), a decade in the writing and his most personal work, is a dynastic novel, broadly in the mode of Mann's *Buddenbrooks* (1901) or Galsworthy's *Forsyte Saga* (1922), which depicts a noble Corfiot family's descent into moral and financial bankruptcy and is pervaded by a very *fin-de-siecle* sense of doom. The elderly count, beleaguered by a Jewish loan-shark and an ambitious doctor, finds himself obliged to barter his two daughters, and after many tragicomical domestic rows goes mad in a scene of King-Lear-like pathos. The deftly caricatured supporting cast of student radicals, ardent mistresses, unemployed *flâneurs*, pompous poetasters and corrupt politicians, without quite making it a *roman à clef*, was sufficiently recognizable to have caused a local stir.

A year after its publication, Theotokis died painfully of stomach cancer at the age of fifty-one, lamenting that he felt he still had another decade's writing in him. He had lived just long enough to witness the demise of the *Megali Idea*, with the humiliating rout of the Greek forces in western Turkey by Mustapha Kemal in 1922 and the ensuing massacre and expulsion of the Greeks from Smyrna. In her tribute to him published in 1927, the poet Eirene Dendrinou observed that, distinguished as his services to modern Greek culture had been as a scholar and translator, it was his own fiction that deserved to be translated.

Theotokis' rustic short stories, almost all first published in the demotic periodical *Noumas* between 1904 and 1914, and edited posthumously by

INTRODUCTION

Dendrinou in 1935 under the title *Corfiot tales*, are among his most powerful works of fiction. Like Maupassant's Normandy stories or Verga's *Life in the fields* (1880) or Hardy's *Wessex tales* (1888), they reflect an intimate knowledge of peasant culture, gleaned in part from his childhood experiences at Karousades, where he felt at home among the villagers. And though less numerous and varied than, for instance, the tales of Skiathos by Papadiamandis, Greece's first professional writer, they are unsentimental, highly crafted and suspenseful, making expert use of *prosa dialogata* to bring the joys and tribulations of his humble protagonists dramatically to life.

As in all his realistic fiction, Theotokis focuses on the primal passions — lust, rage, jealousy, fear, grief, hatred — a universalizing strategy assimilated from Homer, Greek tragedy and Shakespeare which also reflects the influence of Nietzsche, whose theories about the Dionysian irrational were so disturbing to classically educated Europe. Moreover, though they vary in length and range of mood, almost all the tales involve honour and the spectre of revenge, evoking a culture akin to that which survived until recent times in neighbouring Epirus, Albania and Sicily. No doubt this was partly with an eye to catching the attention of the journal's readership, but like class consciousness, piety and superstition, honour and shame were at the epicentre of group psychology in such remote communities. And Theotokis explores their complex controlling influence, particularly in sexual and marital relationships, with a mixture of anthropological detachment, wry humour and compassion. Collectively the *Corfiot tales* portray a closed, clannish, fiercely patriarchal society resistant to change, in which the father, the church and public opinion hold sway, women have few rights, marriages are arranged and life proceeds according to time-honoured rituals against a backdrop of the revolving seasons and the decrees of fate.

The horrific opening story, 'Face down' (1898), has a seminal place in the development of Theotokis' narrative artistry, which gains in depth and subtlety as the volume proceeds. Though conventionally plot-driven, it is strikingly modern in its minimalist directness, showing the implacable workings of the honour code and the powerlessness of women, humanizing the villain with a few deft strokes and answering the *aporia* of the title in the stunning final line. The slightly longer 'Not done yet?' (1904) is on the same theme and similarly structured, but provides a fuller social context, revealing the influence of the extended family when honour is at stake. Both illustrate how effectively Theotokis conveys extreme emotion by describing its physical effects. 'Cain' (1904), a tale which reflects the economic precariousness and mutual dependency of shepherd families, makes the biblical archetype more plausible by internalizing the conflict, presenting the villain's rage and lust for vengeance through his rationalizing inner monologues. The equally sanguinary 'Honourable people' (1905), a first-person oral narrative evoking a world of clan feuding, shows how honour codes, while beyond the pale of church and state, are governed by their own strict principles. 'Village life' (1904) is a more humorous story full of local colour, which reveals how even in matchmaking a father's honour, or *philotimo,* is very much engaged. The rustic scenes of livestock coming home at dusk, of dancing the *syrto,* or of lovemaking to the sound of nightingales are memorable but never mere tableaux, and their potential sentimentality is defused by sobering reflections such as: 'all had forgotten their worries, their barren toil and the bitterness of life and were preparing to enjoy themselves.'

As stories about rivalry in love which focus on the exploitation of peasant women by their masters, 'Reputation' (1904) and 'Stalakti's wedding' (1905) form a diptych, perhaps drawn from Theotokis' personal adventures. Idyllic in setting and at times hilarious, 'Reputation' shows how even the very poorest have their pride, and the heroine's ordeal — parental violence, well-side gossip, an Albanian-style gathering of the clan — exemplifies the kind of restrictions marriageable women were subjected to lest they become 'soiled goods'. 'Stalakti's wedding' (1905), with its mellow harvest scenes, is a darker tale which draws attention to the economic cost of sexual impropriety for women, a theme later resumed in *Honour and cash.* The squire, aided by a wily village pander, becomes attached to the lovely Stalakti, but has to contend with a rabble-rousing rival and the opposition of his own controlling father resident in town. Theotokis' gift for vivid portrayal of the humblest characters is illustrated by the memorable figure of Stalakti's frail courageous comical old dad.

The last three stories are perhaps the most thought-provoking in the volume — 'Illicit love' (1906) in particular, a powerful anguished psychological drama of obsessive lust reminiscent of Tolstoy's *The Devil* (1898). Never revised for publication by Theotokis, and not included in

INTRODUCTION

Dendrinou's 1935 edition of *Corfiot tales*, it confronts the taboo subject of incest, which may well have been an issue in such remote communities, as it appears again in *Hangman Thomas*.[7] A wealth of folkloric detail about Orthodox marriage ceremonies, dowries, traditional costumes and Greek and Italian dancing is presented, again not as tableaux but finely integrated into the dramatic action. And as in almost all the stories, the characters persuade themselves that what happens is their destiny. But unlike Nietzsche or D. H. Lawrence and like the Greek tragedians and Shakespeare, Theotokis tends to see passion as a destructive rather than a liberating force.

'Two loves'(1910) and 'Was it a sin?'(1914) acknowledge the deep piety of such communities, despite the violence, and in both the clergy are positively portrayed, in contrast to *Hangman Thomas*, where the grasping hypocritical priest receives a thorough socialist lambasting. In some respects a synthesis of the earlier tales, 'Two loves' is explicitly about social change, exemplified by the conflict between the icon painter and his son, who asserts his right to choose his own wife and occupation. But it is also about the privileged status of the artist, the dignity of manual labour and the rival claims of art and life within Theotokis' own — as in Yeats' or indeed any artist's — career.[8] And the greater realism of the painter's icons, compared to those of his Byzantine forbears, mirrors Theotokis' gravitation away from the Aestheticism of his early fiction towards the Naturalism of his major work — in apparent agreement with Tolstoy's strictures against 'art for art's sake' in *What is art* (1898). The final scene, in which the 'Annunciation' icon miraculously brings peace, implies an optimistic vision of the role of art in a world where God is dead. In the atmospheric minimalist 'Was it a sin?' an intense inner drama is played out against the stately rituals of the Greek Orthodox church service, as a priest finds himself confronted by a moral and spiritual dilemma. And in answering the question posed in the title, the reader too is prompted to ponder the wider existential problems of the modern era.

---

[7] Freud's Oedipal theories, which focus on unconscious incest and precipitated the rift with Jung, were first made more widely available in *Totem and Taboo* (1913).

[8] 'The intellect of man is forced to choose / Perfection of the life, or of the work', from 'The choice' by W.B. Yeats.

INTRODUCTION

In all his fiction Theotokis followed Solomos and other Ionian writers in using demotic Greek, as against the archaizing *katharevousa* favoured by the intelligentsia in Athens, which imposed classical Greek forms on the vernacular, creating a hybrid officialese that endured until after the demise of the Colonels in 1974, and perpetuated the split between the spoken and the written word that had occurred during the Byzantine era. The development of *katharevousa* was partly a practical matter of the need to standardize and enrich the simpler post-Ottoman spoken language, with its many regional dialects. But it was also a nationalist and class response to the Romantic philhellenes' assumption that the modern Greeks were the descendants of the Homeric heroes — an idea scorned by the German scholar Jakob Fallmerayer, who in 1835 argued that any such tenuous connections had been severed by the Slavic invasions of the Balkans in the seventh century.

Theotokis, like all his contemporaries, was intensely interested in the language question, co-editing a demotic journal, the *Corfiot Anthology*, with Dendrinou and inviting mainland demoticists, including the poet Kostis Palamas, to a symposium in Corfu. His own use of essentially non-dialectal demotic Greek was dictated by linguistic and aesthetic considerations but also by his socialist convictions. And in adapting the techniques of drama, essentially an oral medium, to his Naturalist fiction he was able to showcase the versatility of the spoken language while making his work accessible to a wider readership — felicitously so, since *katharevousa* is no longer taught or used in official documents and newspapers today.

It is ironic therefore, as Dendrinou implied in her 1927 tribute, that so internationally-minded a writer should not until recently have been accessible in English, though two of his novels did appear early on in French, translated by Léon Krajewski as *Le condamné* (1929) and *L'honneur et l'argent* (1933). One or two shorter Corfiot stories have appeared in English anthologies before, but this is the first full English translation of the *Corfiot tales*. As with film adaptations, translations have a de-familiarizing effect for those who know both languages, possibly less so with narrative fiction than with lyric poetry because of the sense of continuity provided by the plot and characters. The attempt here is to present a simulacrum which balances the competing claims of accuracy and idiomatic English, while conveying something of the sinewy directness and rich variety of Theotokis' prose.

The stories make some use of regional vocabulary, but there are fewer exotic imprecations, blessings or kinship terms used as direct forms of address to contend with than in *Hangman Thomas*. Theotokis had a good ear, and one difficulty, especially with the shorter tales, is to avoid making terse pitch-perfect dialogue sound trite. Often the original is so condensed and nuanced that paraphrase is unavoidable: the titles 'Face down', 'Not done yet?' and 'Was it a sin?' for example are all single words in Greek. Theotokis also had a film or theatre director's awareness of his characters' movements, gestures and facial expressions as they speak, and this keeps the translator on his toes as well. The tributes to Corfu's splendid flora and the rustic peasant scenes are often lyrical — in 'Reputation' the girls ascending from the well, their pitchers balanced on their heads, are likened to 'an antique procession of libation bearers making their way to some festive rite' — and pose a poetic challenge. The rhyming couplets in the same story, drawn from and evoking a world of oral balladry, are also tricky to get right. With the more elaborate folkloric descriptions, for instance of Chrysavyi's coiffure in 'Illicit love', the temptation is to simplify; but Theotokis was an ethnographically meticulous observer and the pictorial record often confirms his details. In the two longest tales some of the sentences are of almost Proustian complexity, anticipating the purple passages in *Slaves in their Chains*. In general, his prose is musical, as one might expect of someone brought up speaking Italian, and this is perhaps the hardest thing to emulate successfully.

This translation is based on the Greek text edited by Yannis Dallas, with illustrations by Markos Zavitsianos (Athens: Keimena, 1978), which includes 'Illicit love'. The main sources for the biographical and critical comments in this Introduction are *The early years of Konstantinos Theotokis* by the author's brother Spyridon M. Theotokis (1983), and the standard works by Emilios Chourmouzios and Yannis Dallas — all in Greek, full details in the Bibliography.

I should like to thank George Georghallides for responding to numerous queries, and Anthony Hirst, Jim Potts and my wife Poh Pheng for their invaluable criticism and suggestions.

J. M. Q. Davies, Sydney 2017

FACE DOWN

When, following the anarchy that had convulsed the land, licensing unruly spirits to commit all kinds of lawlessness, order was finally restored and an amnesty declared, the bandits began to return home from the mountains and beyond the seas, among them a certain Andonis Koukouliotis from the village of Magoulades.*

He was approaching forty at the time, a stocky swarthy man with a handsome bushy beard and dark, curly hair. His face was not without charm and his eyes steady and caressing, though with a greenish glint, but his mouth was very small and pinched and almost lipless.

At some time before the people had risen in revolt, this man had married. And when he took to the hills out of fear of the authorities, he had left his wife at home alone; but she had not remained faithful and (perhaps believing Koukouliotis had been killed or met with some other misadventure) taken a lover, giving birth to a child which in due course had become a little charmer and the apple of its mother's eye.

And so one evening at dusk the bandit returned to his village. He entered his home suddenly and without warning when no one was expecting him, like a visitation from the plague, and to the horror of his poor wife, who was so terrified she snatched up her fair-haired child and stood clutching it in her arms and trembling, unable to utter a single word and on the point of fainting.

But Koukouliotis, smiling bitterly, said to her, 'Don't be frightened, woman. I won't harm you, much as you deserve it. Is this your child? Yes? But not mine! Well then tell me, who's the father?'

Sobbing convulsively, she replied, 'Andonis, I can't hide anything from you. I'm greatly to blame. But I know your vengeance will be terrible as well, and I, weak vessel, like this infant trembling with fear, am powerless against you. Look how I'm quaking as I stand before you. Do what you like with me, but pity this poor defenceless creature that has no one to take care of him.'

While the woman was talking his face had darkened, but he did not interrupt her. He remained silent for a moment and then said, 'Wicked woman! I neither asked for your advice nor feel sorry for you and your child. But I want the man's name. You I will not harm. So you won't confess? Well, I'll find out anyway, the whole village knows who you've been living with, and then I'll sacrifice all three of you, I'll wash away the dishonour you have brought on me, you shameless creature!'*

She confessed the name. Koukouliotis left at once. When he returned home hours later, he found the woman still rooted to the spot, clutching the sleeping infant in her arms. She looked at him searchingly, but he stretched out on the ground and, as if satiated, fell into a deep slumber until dawn.

When they awoke next day, he said to her, 'We're going to our fields so I can see if they've seized them too, the way the dead man took you from me.'

'You've killed him!'

That day the sun in the east did not appear, as the sky was overcast and the light struggled to break through the clouds.

Shouldering a spade and hoe, Koukouliotis ordered the woman to follow with the child and all three left the house.

On reaching the field, which was still moist following some recent rain, the bandit set about digging a hole.

He did not say a word, his face was pale and a chill sweat poured from his brow. The wan light filtering through the clouds gave a weird complexion to the scene: that grey autumnal morning summed up all his grief. The woman looked on with anxious curiosity, while the toddler played with the sods the ruthless man was turning over. For a fleeting moment the sun came out, gilding the child's flaxen hair as it smiled angelically.

By now the hole was ready and, leaning on his spade, Koukouliotis told his wife, 'Put it in. Face down.'

Krasades, November 1898

NOT DONE YET?

The millstone was revolving. Two logs glowed faintly amid the thick smoke from the hearth. The mill ground steadily, the press extruded oil.* Three of the mill-hands were at work, two others sleeping on the ground on piles of waste. It was midnight and quite chilly.

The door opened and a huntsman entered with his dogs. He was a tall man of about forty with a calm but manly face, clad in a woollen jacket, baggy trousers and a fez. He seemed upset.

'Good evening, Theodosis,' they said. 'Out shooting ferrets?'

'Good evening,' he replied. 'Where's Kourkoupos?'

'He's sleeping over there,' said one of the hands, a middle-aged man who was, as they say, captain of the mill. Then he added, 'Kourkoupos, wake up. It's your cousin.'

But Kourkoupos was dead to the world and did not stir. Theodosis went over and nudged him with his foot.

'What's up?' he asked, still half asleep. 'I've only just dossed down. My shift again already?'

'Wake up, your wife wants you. I was out ferreting and saw her.'

Alarmed, Kourkoupos got to his feet at once.

He was a young man of about twenty-five, not handsome, but with a kindly good-natured look about him. He too was wearing rustic clothes, greasy with oil, and he was a little hunched from his incessant labour.

The two men left together. The village was asleep. The stars lit up the road. Now and then a dog would bark at them.

'What's the matter?' asked Kourkoupos in trepidation.

His companion did not reply. Silently they hurried on until they reached their neighbourhood. Kourkoupos ran up to his house but found the door bolted on the outside.

'Where is she?' he asked, ashamed.

'Over at Ermones,'* Theodosis replied, and without another word he set off down the hill. His companion followed; his limbs were drenched in a cold sweat and his back was freezing; he had completely lost the power of speech.

NOT DONE YET?

They descended the narrow path toward the sea. The scene was desolate. At that late hour, the steep rugged hills loomed darkly; the water in the stream seethed over the stones. At Gallows Fork* they stopped and hid behind a rock. Kourkoupos' knees were trembling so much he had to sit down; his companion looked at him sharply, trying to make out his expression in the dark. They waited, listening intently.

The sails of the windmills turned incessantly and the singing of the mill-hands reached their ears, mingling with the sound of running water and the first crowing of the cocks.

Suddenly the dogs began to growl, but Theodosis silenced them and whispered, 'There she is. Here, take this!' And he thrust his gun into his cousin's hand.

A shadowy figure was coming up the hill towards them. Mechanically, Kourkoupos took the gun and cocked it. His eyes were riveted to the person hurrying towards them. Not a sound came from the dogs. Kourkoupos heaved a sigh of relief and lowered his weapon, saying, 'It's a man!'

'It's her, dressed as a man, the dogs have recognized her. Shoot!'

He did not obey, reluctant to believe it.

'It's her, dressed as a man, I tell you,' his companion repeated impatiently. 'I saw her on her way down.'

And with these words he extinguished his cousin's last remaining hope. Inwardly Kourkoupos now realized that he was destined to become a murderer, and the thought so terrified the good man that it eclipsed both his anger and his grief.

Meanwhile she had hurried past them and was on the point of disappearing round the bend.

'What are you waiting for? She'll get away. It's her, I tell you,' said Theodosis in a hoarse voice. 'You've both dishonoured us.' And he tried to snatch the gun from him.

'It's not for you to kill her!' replied his cousin and steeling his resolve he shouted, 'Stop, woman, or else . . .'

But she started running as fast as her heels would carry her and in a moment had disappeared from view.

'You see, you see? She's getting away, the shameless slut,' cried Theodosis.

The two of them set off after her at once, the dogs barking as they joined in the chase.

Rounding the bend they again caught sight of her not far ahead. Kourkoupos, by now enraged, shouted out, 'Stop, stop.' His companion kept urging him, 'Shoot! Have done with it!'

But Kourkoupos paid no attention; he now wanted to hear from her own lips that she had dishonoured him and ran on; he managed to outflank her and catch up with her at the edge of the village and, seizing her by the hair, forced her to the ground.

She let out a piercing scream.

'Not here,' Theodosis muttered, 'the whole village will wake up. Give me the gun so you're not caught red-handed.'

Kourkoupos obeyed and relinquished the weapon; then seizing the terrified woman with both hands he dragged her home.

With a chilly heart she opened the door herself, as she had the keys, and the couple entered alone together. He slammed the door violently behind them.

For a moment they stood there in the dark, both of them afraid. But then out of habit she added some kindling to the fire still smouldering in the hearth, and at once the room lit up.

Kourkoupos' face was thunderous; looking at him the woman felt faint and sat down on the floor.

She seemed smaller in the man's clothing that betrayed her guilt; looking at her he was consumed with rage and his mind went dark, and after a moment's silence he heaved a deep sigh and said, 'Down at Ermones at this hour dressed as a man! What have you been up to, bitch?'

She didn't say a word. Then with a shudder he made the fateful decision. Casting his eye around the room he caught sight of a chisel and at once grabbed hold of it. In a flash he was beside her, repeating menacingly, 'What have you been up to? What have you been up to?'

And the longer she remained silent from sheer terror and remorse, the more his fury mounted and the more he tormented her, until finally the hapless creature realized that her hour had come.

'Mercy, mercy,' she cried, 'I have sinned, but I am pregnant; I swear to God, the child is yours!'

Kourkoupos turned pale and hesitated; what she had said disarmed him.

The fire had dwindled and she was weeping fervently; outside, dawn was breaking.

Theodosis, who had been waiting, knocked violently on the door and cried, 'Not done yet? Not done yet?'

And as if in answer, piercing screams came from within, 'Mercy, have pity on your child. Inhuman brute, you've killed me!' Then at the top of her lungs, 'Help, help! . . . Ah!'

Complete silence followed.

But then the nearby houses opened up and the neighbours emerged, half dressed and much perturbed, men and children assembling in front of Kourkoupos' house to find out what was going on, only to be greeted by a stifled gurgling coming from within.

Theodosis answered them, 'He's killed her.'

Krasades, January 1904.

CAIN

Kostas Lambouras returned home that evening deeply upset. His face was livid, his eyes restless and protruding and his thin lips bloodless, giving him an ugly, savage and alien expression. His fez sat awry upon his head, his cloak was thrown carelessly over one shoulder and his shirtsleeves were dirty and unbuttoned.

Inside, his wife was cooking supper and upon entering he went and sat down by the hearth, as the chilly autumn weather had set in already. He was breathing heavily and did not greet her, and now and then he would jerk his head aggressively.

'What are you cooking, Evyenia?' he asked her in a surly voice.

'Vegetables,' she replied, glancing at him anxiously. 'What's up now?'

'He's ruined us!' he replied sighing moodily. 'He's returned the flock to the landlord. How are we supposed to make a living?'

'But Kostas,' she ventured gently, 'it was only rented. Keeping up the payments wasn't easy, and you resented doing so, so how could he have kept it?' And she smiled.

'What'd you mean?' he replied giving her a sour look. 'Who taught you to think like that? No one pays up these days. What had he to fear?'

'The law's the law. They'd have slapped you both in jail, and your brother's not keen on doing time.'

'Jail over such trivial things,' he replied scornfully. 'As if they jailed people just like that! D'you think the bad old days are here again! That's all over and done with. Nowadays everyone does as he pleases. What do we elect M.P.s for? Our own convenience, of course.* Who ever asked a favour without receiving it? Murders are reported every day, but how long do the investigations take? Months! And yet my lordly brother got cold feet. What could they have done, repossessed the flock? Over my dead body! But I'll soon straighten out that fine brother of mine!'

He fell silent and his expression grew fiercer as he continued brooding. Yes, his brother had indeed wronged him. What right had he to hand back the flock just now in winter when they had no other means. But then why should his brother give a damn — unmarried, childless, carefree, whom had he to feed? Only his own carcass. Once poverty overtook them he'd be able to escape, leaving them to battle in the cold against hunger and privation. He'd be able to earn a crust anywhere because he was no shirker. But what would he himself do then, how would he provide for his family? He had always been a lazy fellow. The olive trees were not yielding much these days. Only the flock would see them through the year. And now his brother, be it out of malice or stupidity, had returned it to the landlord. Ah, he had indeed acted like his enemy!

Evyenia was stirring the vegetables in the pot. She tasted them, got up and took some bread down from a hanging-basket, then, looking her husband in the eyes, said nervously, 'The food is ready.'

'I'm not hungry,' he answered rudely; and went on ruminating bitterly, 'He left without my even suspecting. True, he mentioned it the other day but I thought it was just talk. I didn't think he'd dare. Ah, if I'd known, there's no way I'd have let him do it. I'd have challenged him and slaughtered him. But he deceived me. I fondly imagined he had my best interests at heart, that he was under my thumb and happy to be working for our family. He insisted almost daily that he wasn't interested in marriage, and everybody said he was devoted to me. Now he's suddenly become cocksure and done the first thing that came into his head, the very thing I didn't want. He didn't consider the worries it would cause us, even though he knew my family and I would suffer, because he's confident he can make a living anywhere. But what's the use? He got round me and gave me the slip. No point in brooding and lamenting. It won't bring back my flock. Our fate is sealed. Come winter we will starve to death! Did I say winter? Already by tomorrow we'll be out of bread. But he's always been against me. When he wasn't trying to stop me marrying Evyenia — and I did so just to spite him — he'd be watching to see I didn't steal, or cheat, or commit some other crime, always interfering, always ill-disposed towards me. That's why we never got along. Not a day went by when I didn't curse him. And now he's done this to me. But I'll show him when he returns tomorrow. Yes, he'll soon see! He won't return of course. He'll be too scared. He'll have scuttled off abroad. Just as well for him, because he'd have made me become a . . .'

His eyes widened and he shuddered at the terrifying thought.

'Let's go to bed,' said his wife. 'Don't get so worked up, Kostas, it's a sin.'

He looked at her blankly, as if waking from a nightmare. 'Go and lie down, I'll come and join you soon,' he said to her abstractedly. But she didn't move.

'Cain!' said a voice deep within him, 'Do you intend to kill your own brother? Even if he is responsible for this disaster, he is still your brother. You live together, sprang from the same womb, suckled the same milk, have the same blood, share the same bread, have been together since you first saw the light of day.' And in his mind he replied, 'But I must punish him, satisfy my appetite for vengeance. He deserves it. He has beggared me, ruined me completely.' And the voice from the depths of his being answered, 'Cain, aren't you afraid? How can you harbour such dark thoughts in your heart? What, shed your own blood, become a dishonourable murderer?'

'He deserves it,' he brooded. 'He's treated me abominably and I shall be even worse. A savage beast, a tiger. He deserves it because he's ruined me completely. Let the landlord save him if he can. We'll soon see.' And the voice replied, 'Do you not fear God? Do you not fear the gallows?' 'The gallows,' he thought derisively, 'the gallows, in this day and age? What are our M.P.s for? The party too will act on my behalf, the party is all-powerful. What court is going to try me? And if it convicts me, the party will get me off the hook. Woe to him who loses everything. I'm a ruined man, so let my brother be destroyed as well. Even if they catch me in the end, there's not much they can do to me. Besides, they might never catch me.'

To his wife he said, 'I'm going to kill him.'

Dumbfounded, she stood up and looked at him in disbelief, but quickly averted her eyes when she saw the ruthless determination in his face.

'What harm has your good brother done you?' she said.

'Good? What d'you mean, good?' he replied getting to his feet in a rage. 'He's starving us to death! What? So you're siding with him, are you, you old baggage? I will kill him!'

'Oh God, what monstrous wickedness,' she sobbed. 'They'll hang you, Cain!'

Stunned, Kostas Lambouras looked round at his wife. He had just heard the self-same voice from her lips that had been speaking to him from the depths of his own being. How could she know his secret thoughts, his soul's clarion cry of protest? And suddenly his unruly imagination conjured up a terrifying scene. He had already committed the murder and, still holding the bloody knife, was fleeing through the centre of the village, where everyone stared at him aghast and then turned away, contemptuously uttering the accursed name of Adam's firstborn: 'Cain, it's Cain!' From then on his wife too took to calling him by that name. But the villagers did not know how his evil brother had mistreated him. They didn't realize that he'd been wronged. All they could see was the murder and so condemned him. Kostas wanted to reply: 'My brother brought his fate upon himself. He signed his own death sentence. Anyone in my predicament would have killed — even his own father if he were that unjust. Who obliged me to become another Cain? Why, my brother himself. A Cain yes, but an avenger, a punisher, an upholder of justice. No, I don't seek praise, good people, but look more closely and understand my deed. You envy me and fear me for my daring. Yes, good people, you fear me and through fear I shall control you!'

By now his seething blood was cooling down. 'Better for nobody to know,' he told himself, 'and I'll make sure they don't. I'll kill him secretly, under cover of darkness, in the dead of night. But kill him I must.'

'Let's get some sleep,' he told his wife more calmly. 'Go and make the bed.'

'You frighten me,' she replied trembling.

'Why? I'm not going to harm you. Let's get some sleep.'

Inwardly he felt a certain satisfaction; he had hardened his heart and made his decision. His mind had become accustomed to all these inhuman thoughts. He was himself aware that by killing he would be gratifying some inner craving, some thirst that only blood could quench. How sweet this exemplary revenge he was considering, this payback for injustice, felt.

And consumed with a hatred that again set his blood boiling and made him see red, he stretched out beside his wife, who had withdrawn as far over to her side as possible, and fell into a fitful sleep haunted by terrifying dreams of carnage — knives, guns, fighting, disembowelments — and often a groan would issue from his chest and he would shake with fear.

But meanwhile his plan continued to ripen in his ruthless heart.

The very next afternoon, Nikolas Lambouras arrived back by caique — the village of Lefkoraki was not far from the sea. In town he had seen to his business with the landlord, handed over the flock, payed what they owed, and was now returning with a sack full of tasty provisions for his brother's family and what cash remained. When he reached home, Kostas was still out and Evyenia was hard at work in the garden. Anxiously she ran to meet him before he could cross the threshold and, without pausing to greet him, cried excitedly, 'Poor wretch, why have you come back?'

'What's up?' he asked, turning round unsuspectingly and gazing at her with his innocent eyes.

'He's made up his mind, he's going to kill you.'

'Who?'

'Your brother.'

'Whatever for?' he asked her smiling. 'Don't believe it. Kostas is a good man.'

'Ah, Nikolas,' she sighed, 'I swear by your ancestors it's true. I beg you, for my sake, leave before he sees you. He's made up his mind to do you in. I've seen the malice in his eyes. He's outraged that you returned the flock.'

'The flock? But it wasn't ours. I explained this to him just the other day. The landlord put me in charge of it while Kostas was away in jail and I returned it. True, Kostas wanted me to hold on to it, but he didn't raise objections. His anger will blow over as it always does. God will provide for us. Times are hard but we'll get by, we'll find other work.'

'I know you're right, Nikolas, but as you value your life, flee. Save yourself and save us all. There was malice in his eyes, I tell you. Any minute he'll be back and then you're a dead man.'

'Evyenia, I simply don't believe it,' he said smiling again. 'He's just letting off steam, you'll see.' He entered the house and sat down by the hearth, in the very place where his brother had been sitting on the previous evening.

Anxiously Evyenia followed him.

'I'm hungry,' he declared.

'I tremble for you both,' she replied.

'Stop frightening yourself and bring me some bread,' he said good-naturedly.

She obeyed and then sat down in her corner deep in thought. As he ate, Nikolas recounted how the good landlord had welcomed him, how they had done their accounts and he had received a bonus, and what else they had discussed; then he went on to talk about the town, his purchases, his tavern meal and the people he had seen, and so time passed. But all the while anxiety was gnawing at Evyenia's vitals. Any minute now her husband would return and then who could tell what might happen in their home. She didn't hear a word of what Nikolas was saying, as she sat there with tears in her eyes, sighing frequently.

Dusk had fallen when Kostas returned home; there was venom in his look but he controlled himself and greeted them.

'Good evening,' he said, 'and welcome back.'

Evyenia thought of throwing herself at his feet and begging him for mercy, but she was too frightened, again detecting malice in his eyes. Nikolas replied warmly, 'Good evening, brother. Business went well. I've brought back these few provisions and a bit of cash.'

'How much?'

'Ten fivers.'*

'Was that all the flock was worth?'

'No. That was our wage.'

'Well, what's done is done,' replied Kostas smiling sourly and then scowled.

They said no more after that and all three settled round the hearth — Kostas brooding, Nikolas half asleep and Evyenia gazing nervously now at one and now the other. The hours slipped by. By now it was the dead of night.

Suddenly the dog barked; at once Kostas remarked, 'Perhaps it heard the dog from the flock we returned barking.'

'Yes,' said Nikolas waking up, 'it must still be out there somewhere.'

'No, someone's passing by. I'd better take a look. Who could it be at this late hour?' And Kostas got up and went outside.

'You see, Evyenia,' said Nikolas smiling, 'it was all a passing hailstorm. Tomorrow everything will be milk and honey.'

'Don't trust him,' she pleaded. 'I don't like the look in his eye. His heart is black.'

'Nikolas, Nikolas,' came Kostas' voice from outside, 'it's some folk in trouble. Let's help them out. Smugglers on the beach near Kalami.* The police are onto them and they stand to lose their goods.'

'Don't go, don't go!' pleaded the woman.

'You're starting at shadows, Evyenia. Why are you so scared? How can I refuse to help them get away? Can't you hear how the dogs are carrying on. Someone must surely have approached.'

'No, there are flocks near by. Don't go! Don't go!'

'I won't listen to any more of this,' he answered and went out.

Then Evyenia felt a pang of anguish rend her heart.

It was a moonless night but a myriad stars lit up the sky; the air was still and one could hear the monotonous booming of the sea. 'Down there,' said Kostas pointing, 'near Kalami. Let's hurry,' and he set off at a brisk pace. Nikolas followed close at his heels.

They did not say a word on the way down and soon they reached the shore.

'Well, where are they?' Nikolas asked.

'Over there by the jetty under the cliff,' replied his brother.

The bay was fringed with a sandy pebble-strewn beach and the waves gently lapping it were black as ink. They proceeded swiftly towards the cliff which rose sheer out of the sea, forming an insuperable barrier between the Lefkoraki beach and the one beyond, but here too there was no sign of any smugglers or caique, and suddenly Nikolas became alarmed and recalled his sister-in-law's fears. Shaken, he demanded, 'Well, where are they?'

'Who? . . . I brought you here to slit your throat.'

Then his hapless brother realized that he was doomed; with a scream he flung himself on Kostas in an attempt to grab his wrists, yelling out, 'Cain! Help, help!'

Only the echoes answered. Kostas stepped back into the sea, enraged by his brother's curse, which stung him like a whiplash, and alarmed by his clamorous screams, which were already betraying his intentions. Then quick as a flash he pulled out a pistol and emptied it into his brother's chest, exclaiming, 'Take that, inhuman brute, you've beggared us.'

Nikolas reeled and collapsed into the surf, still calling out 'Cain, Cain, help!' for he was only wounded. But his cries outraged the villain, who put his hand over his mouth, drew a dagger from his belt and, averting his gaze, plunged it repeatedly into his brother, inflicting several lethal wounds. But still the wretched man did not expire, as the blade had entered obliquely and failed to pierce either his heart or neck; a hollow groan came from his mangled chest as he writhed in agony in the dark waters.

Suddenly the sound of barking dogs and the cries of people heading for the shore rang out; Kostas at once realized that the shepherds must have heard the screams and pistol shots and were coming to the rescue; in a panic he hastened to conceal himself, leaving his brother behind in the water more dead than alive.

'Where are you? We're coming!' two voices shouted, in response to which a faint groan came from the expiring man.

Kostas calculated that by now the shepherds would have reached his brother and, fearing his victim might betray him, scrambled from his hiding place and hurried towards him too. The shepherds, all carrying lanterns, their dogs leading the way, had not yet reached the cliff; but by now the hideous groans were distinctly audible above the sound of the waves. Everyone hurried on in silence and at last they reached the scene. On first catching sight of his brother's pitiable body lashed by the blood-stained surf, Kostas covered his eyes with his hands. But quickly recovering, he flung himself upon his brother, who by this stage had lost consciousness, and began wailing and beating his chest in lamentation.

The shepherds recognized the victim and deeply moved exclaimed, 'There's been a murder. It's Nikolas Lambouras. Bear up, Kostas.'

'Hurry,' the murderer urged them tearfully, 'fetch people from the village to help carry him; summon the police, a priest, whatever's needed. He is still alive!'

Obediently the shepherds hurried off, leaving a lantern behind, and the two brothers found themselves alone together.

And now the Voice again spoke up from the depths of Kostas' being. 'Cain,' it said, 'you've been as good as your word; now relish your deed.' Fearfully the murderer considered how best to save himself and his first thought was to flee, but his brother was still alive and might betray him, so he resolved to finish him off once and for all and thereby escape punishment and shame. He took out his knife. But the pathetic spectacle of the wounded man prevented him carrying out his intention, and he accidentally knocked over and put out the light. But now the very wounds he had himself inflicted seemed to glow, the bloodstained surf too seemed to be glowing, and the knife fell from his hand.

Just then a sigh came from the dying man.

'Brother,' Kostas said to him, 'forgive me.'

'Accursed Cain,' replied his brother faintly, 'why have you killed me? The gallows now awaits you.'

'No, no, don't denounce me. You're a good man and will find it in your soul. You're not going to die. My wife will nurse you. I'll call in doctors. I'll sell everything we have. I'll look after you till you recover, only don't betray me.'

The dying man groaned and replied, 'You've tortured me. You've stained your hands with fraternal blood. What a calamity you've brought upon our family. Didn't you consider that our mother's bosom suckled both of us, that we were both conceived by the same father?' He attempted to rise but fell back into the waves in agony.

'I repent, I tell you. I could finish you off if I wanted to. I could make sure you never uttered another word. But I haven't the heart. Don't betray me.'

'Whether I live or die, I won't say a word,' replied his anguished brother weeping. 'Why should I destroy your family as well? Cain, let God be your judge!' And he lapsed into unconsciousness again.

Meanwhile several villagers had arrived on the scene; all lamented the attempt on Nikolas Lamboura's life, deeply shocked by the unexpected crime.

They carried him home, wincing with pain. Evyenia, who had not yet gone to bed, came screaming out into the road, all too aware of what had happened. She looked round for her husband and rushing up to him, whispered in his ear, 'Cain, you're as good as your word, I see!' Then she showed the bearers where to lay the dying man.

Kostas sat down outside his own front door, unable to face his brother's mortal struggle. A middle-aged villager washed the wounds with wine and vinegar and bandaged them, but declared that Nikolas would be dead by morning. Then everyone left to go to bed. All night Nikolas lay there without uttering a word and only towards morning opened his eyes again. Then Evyenia approached him and said, 'Nikolas, bless your soul, don't denounce him, don't ruin me as well.'

The dying man shook his head and as he clasped her hand, a sad smile appeared on his withered lips. Then he requested the last rites.

Finally, after the sun had risen, the authorities arrived to interrogate the victim and the others. Kostas once again became terrified lest his brother denounce him and regretted not having dispatched him on the beach. It occurred to him that then his brother had vowed to keep quiet out of fear, and now might reveal everything. So he rushed into the house, fell on his knees before the dying man and started weeping and lamenting. The victim, asked by the magistrate if he had recognized the murderer, shook his head, but when Evyenia saw the complacent smile on her husband's lips she could control herself no longer. Revulsion at this perfidious man welled up within her; her heart cried out for justice and revenge; she realized that she would be spending the rest of her life with this unworthy brute and resolved to sentence him herself. Suddenly, in the presence of the officials, she started screaming, 'Accursed Cain, you're the one who killed him. You and no one else, for all your tears, you treacherous monster.'

Everyone looked at her in stunned amazement, then turned to the expiring man, whose eyes were brimming with tears, and the magistrate asked him: 'is it true?'

There was a deathly silence.

'Don't protect him,' cried the woman. 'Tomorrow he'll murder me as well because I have borne witness.'

The man at death's door nodded, and shortly afterwards gave up the ghost.

Krasades, October 1904

VILLAGE LIFE

Petros Kladis, a peasant landowner from the village of Xacherades, was waiting impatiently at home that afternoon. From his window he would frequently look down the street to see if the man he was expecting was among the few people passing by, and sighed complacently when he finally caught sight of Spyros Stratis, an elderly fellow villager, approaching and entering his door. He received him with a smile.

'Welcome, good matchmaker,' he said at once. 'Doubtless they said yes, so you'll have earned those shoes I promised you.'

The newcomer frowned, looked thoughtful for a moment and then replied sadly, 'I don't know what to say, Petros. I did my best but without success. The shame is as much mine as yours.'

'Ah, you're pulling my leg,' replied the other, flushing. 'What family in the village would refuse to give their daughter to my only son? Everyone knows the lad is young, well provided for and handsome.'

'They said no, I swear to God! Believe me or not as you wish. Indeed the charming Margarita herself told me your son looks like a monkey. She won't have him.'

Petros took the insult very much to heart and was incensed.*

'What,' he shouted, 'my son a monkey? He's a hundred times superior to her. She's unworthy even of his droppings!'

'Yesterday after you sent me I went round to Handrinos's place and told him what I'd come about. Then I called on them again today to receive their answer. The father was keen from the word go and got all fired up, the mother even more so. But that spoiled girl flatly refused to either see or hear from him. The three of us tried in vain to talk her round. She remained as obstinate as a Jew about his faith.'

'She won't even see my son, ay? What's she heard against him?' Petros exclaimed, adding sarcastically, 'Ah, she's not one for getting married honourably, decked out in finery. She'd rather bed the bridegroom first and then consent. Well, she'll get what she wished for, don't you worry. That's the way girls are these days. But she's not the only pebble on the beach. I'll find my son a better match elsewhere, far better.'

'Absolutely. And send me anywhere you wish, even into town.'

Petros made no reply; then after a moment's reflection he said, 'As for your good self, Spyros, it's not your fault that they said no. You've done what I requested, so take your shoes anyway, seeing as I've purchased them. But remember, the Handrinoses are going to pay for this.'

The old man accepted the gift, wishing him long life, then bade him good evening and departed looking glum. Left alone, Petros began to brood, pacing up and down the large whitewashed room, the only room in the house, which had neither window-panes nor ceiling and no furniture besides a large bed and two carved chests against the wall.

'They've caught me on the back foot, those crafty stupid Handrinoses,' he said to himself. 'Full of surprises, that little Miss Margo. And there was I thinking I'd again secured a solid asset for my family. The match would really have been perfect for my son. The girl has both a house and land, a proper little heiress. Quite a beauty too. And she seemed so modest, so innocent, so honest. By Saint Spyridon,* I don't understand the world any more. Why should she refuse us? Where am I going to find another girl as suitable. And I ought to marry the lad off soon, as I'm afraid he might leave the district. Young people like to travel these days and easily forget their native village. Well, I'll do my best, but all in good time. If the matchmaker is to be believed (and isn't trying to deceive me), it's Margarita who disdains us. Her parents would be only too pleased. How could they do better? The Almighty be praised, thanks to my hard work, shrewdness, enterprise and business deals, I've put by something in this world. What my father left me won't be the only thing I pass on to my son. I've tilled, extended and enriched my land, so I won't go short of a crust and neither will he. The Handrinoses know all this. Besides, I've never done them any harm. So it's the girl who won't play ball, no doubt about it, spoiled little minx, humiliating people! But why? A buxom lass like her, how can she not want to get married? There's a fly in the ointment somewhere. Someone has outsmarted me — won her heart behind her parents' back. If I knew who it was and could be sure it was quite innocent and her honour still intact, I might be able to fix things and bring her into the family. But better not, perhaps. What's the sense in bringing home one of those she-devils who make eyes at other men. Beware of women who flash their eyes at you. Myself, I can't abide them. But then again, am I supposed to just forget about the insult? No way, and if the Handrinoses ever fall into my clutches, I'll make their life a misery. Miss Margo will pay dearly for all this. If her father ever owed me money, I would roast him in the courts, but for now I shall be patient.'

Meanwhile evening had set in; more people were now passing along the village street: men returning from the valley in small clusters, women and young lasses laughing together as they goaded on their flocks, and the chatter of the crowd and bleating of the animals wafted in through Petros' window with the sun's last crimson rays.

Petros leaned back out of the window, resting his elbows on the marble sill, and waited for his family to appear. Soon he spotted his wife and two daughters slowly trudging towards the village with their livestock — a pair of sleek black well-fed oxen, tossing their curved horns to shoo away the flies and lowing now and then, several sheep, a goat, some pigs and a packhorse laden with a plough. In amongst his animals were others that belonged to strangers. But as they approached, his separated out and stopped beside the house as they had been trained to, while the rest continued on their way. Then the women swiftly opened the doors to the sheds beside the house and stood urging the animals to enter. Casually they crossed the threshold, the large ones first, moving languidly, followed by the smaller ones, clustering together and jostling each other, until all of them had disappeared into the dark. The women put down their bundles, unloaded the packhorse, drove it into the shed as well and tethered it, shouting instructions to one another, then re-emerged and closed the doors. The girls then went into the kitchen on the ground floor to light a fire, and their mother came upstairs. She was a tall stout rather ugly middle-aged peasant, but that evening her face glowed with a good-natured smile. She quietly bade her husband good evening and sat down on one of the chests, mopping her brow. Petros responded with a nod and looked at her in some embarrassment. Suspecting the reason she gazed at him anxiously and asked, 'Did the matchmaker bring you their answer?'

'Your son looks like a monkey,' Petros replied bluntly. 'That is what the Handrinoses think. Margarita will not have him.'

'Did she really say no?' exclaimed the woman in amazement. 'Well, to hell with her and her ambitions.'

Then after a moment's consideration she continued, 'The worst of it is that for the last few days the girls and I have talked of nothing else but our son's marriage. The whole village knows we wanted him to marry Margarita, and now we'll be a laughing-stock.'

'We'll soon fix that,' he replied thoughtfully, 'all you need say is that I took against the match, as I didn't wish to be burdened with her father's debts. He who laughs last, laughs longest. Anyway, let's not discuss the matter further. Tell me, anything to report from down the valley?'

'No,' she replied glumly, 'the men worked in the field and we grazed the sheep near Handrinos's hut. In fact the girls even talked to Margarita, but they didn't mention anything to me. Dimitris Lazos also came by a couple of times and stopped to watch her planting cabbages; could there be something going on between them?'

'No, no,' piped up one of Petros' daughters, a slight, dishevelled village lass of fifteen just coming up the stairs, 'she's not in love with Dimitris, he's forever pestering her. I think she fancies Markos Saïttas. They've known each other for a while now. She told me so herself.'

'Markos Saïttas,' said Petros with a smile, 'she'll never marry him.'

It was a Sunday during Carnival.* The village churches had rung the bells for Vespers early, since, as every year, there was to be a dance that afternoon. And now after the short service the villagers had already begun to assemble round the dance floor, the men on one side of the square, the women on the other. All had had their fill of good food and wine that day and were in a cheerful mood, all had forgotten their worries, their barren toil and the bitterness of life and were preparing to enjoy themselves. The women, looking spruce, well-kempt and smiling in their Sunday best and (where they had any) their trinkets, chatted quietly amongst themselves; and with their clean, gold-braided costumes, gold necklaces and radiant faces they lent a happy festive air to the village scene, as if no one there had ever known misfortune. Standing in the middle of the dance-floor were the fiddlers and the drummer, while opposite the women a large group of men had gathered — though by no means all those in the village, as others were sauntering about, or slipping into wine-stores for a drink or entertaining their companions with a song.

Now the church bells were ringing and the general merriment and laughter steadily increased, while the drum beat rhythmically, inviting those who felt in the mood to dance. The women adjusted their costumes, each anxious to be placed in the front row by the leader of the dance, and everyone waited eagerly for the proceedings to commence. The fiddlers struck up the monotonous tune of the *syrto*,* while at the same time stepping now forward, now back, to the rhythm of the music. Everybody watched but no one made a move, not game enough to take the initiative uninvited and begin the dance. Several minutes went by like this. Then a tall handsome middle aged man in smart new baggy trousers suddenly appeared. It was the deputy mayor. The instruments fell silent; the women stood waiting, instinctively checking that their headscarves were securely pinned, adjusting their skirts and glancing down at the gold trinkets on their bosoms. Then the deputy mayor approached them, each now holding out a gaily coloured hanky, and picked the girls he fancied, the prettier ones, the more lavishly adorned, or those from his own clan, gathering their tokens and tying them together and assembling some fifteen women in a row on one side of the dance-floor. The dance was ready to begin. The leading female pulled the hankies taut, her companions each placed one hand upon them, the fiddles struck up their monotonous tune again and the drum resounded. The leading male then grasped the string of hankies at mid-point and, dancing forward a few steps, led the women out and then released them; they continued moving rhythmically forward, serious, silent, their eyes downcast, taking two diagonal steps forward, two short steps back, always advancing on the same foot; together they followed the leading male, who now began leaping in front of each of them in turn all down the line, pirouetting and criss-crossing his legs with hands on hips to show off his skill; and soon several other men were dancing with equal vigour alongside him, having joined in to lend him their support. The dance proceeded round the floor to the same monotonous tune, the women moving as one body, never breaking rank and gazing at the ground with modesty and discipline. After a quarter of an hour or so, the fiddles and the drum came to a halt and everyone stopped dancing; the leading dancer saluted the women with a flourish of his fez, before paying the musicians. The women withdrew to their side of the floor, while the men who had joined the dance repaired to a wine-store to cool down. The first dance was now over and the fiddlers began to tune their instruments in preparation for the second.

Now Dimitris Lazos hurried over to the women, anxious lest someone else get there before him, and began gathering their hankies. He was a slight, swarthy young man with shifty eyes. He chose a female lead, then looked about to see if Margarita Handrinos were there, and on spotting her asked her for her hanky. But the girl snubbed him, turning away and pretending not to hear him. Dimitris flushed red and glared at her a moment: she was a young lass of eighteen, with unusually refined features and a beautiful complexion, and her woollen dress was simple and immaculate, but like the rest of the unmarried women she was not wearing any jewellery. Then suddenly abashed by her good looks, he turned away with feigned indifference, selected other women and led off the dance.

Petros Kladis, who was looking on from the crowd, noticed all of this. 'Well, well, so she refused him. What my daughter said was true then!' and he shook his head as he reflected on the dancer's humiliation. The latter meanwhile, having completed a dance much like the first one, withdrew and joined the spectators. Petros Kladis followed him with his eyes, then gradually worked his way towards him and greeted him casually. The third dance was led by a young man who had a reputation in the village for his dancing prowess and the fourth by Petros' son, but Margarita did not favour either with her token. Then, Markos Saïttas, a lithe and handsome youth, approached the women, and on him Margarita did smilingly bestow her hanky, whereupon he placed her second in line next to the lead dancer. The instruments struck up and the dance again got under way.

Then with an ironic smile, Petros Kladis muttered in Dimitris' ear, 'She's not interested in you, poor fellow, look at the way she smiles at Markos. You're wasting your time.'

Markos meanwhile was dancing with manly vigour, nimbly crisscrossing his legs, pirouetting and leaping in the air before the women; but whenever he found himself opposite Margarita he would summon all his skill and dance even more enchantingly, showing off his most artful figures. Dimitris seethed with jealous rage.

But this dance too came to an end. In the wine-stores people went on drinking and carousing, while round the dance floor the spectators praised or criticized the women, their costumes, their gold trinkets, their complexions and their dancing. Two or three more dances followed and by now dusk had fallen. To round things off, Markos wanted to gather the tokens one last time.

At this Petros Kladis whispered in Dimitris' ear, 'He's taken her from under your nose. You'd think he was the only one dancing here tonight.'

Stung, Dimitris rushed over to the women, grabbed the tokens Markos had begun to tie, declaring angrily, 'I'm leading this dance.'

'I've already gathered up the hankies,' replied Markos firmly.

'I'll relieve you of them!'

The two men eyed each other fiercely; the women went pale and shrank back a little, and the villagers could see there was going to be trouble. But for the moment no one felt sufficiently alarmed to leave.

'What,' said Markos angrily, 'd'you think I'm not man enough then? D'you think I'm going to ask a rat like you permission to dance?' And he gave Dimitris a violent shove.

At this the women immediately broke line and prepared to leave; there was a general stir among the crowd; many gathered round the quarrelling men, some asserting that Dimitris was in the right, others supporting Markos, and all the time the commotion steadily increased. The more prudent looked on sadly, anticipating bloodshed. But Petros Kladis, seeing that matters had developed just the way he wanted, now intervened and as the crowd respected him it quietened down to hear what he would say. In a loud commanding voice he announced, 'The musicians may now leave, there'll be no more dancing.' Then grabbing Dimitris by the arm he scolded him severely, saying, 'This is no way to behave. Look how you've upset the whole village with your fit of jealousy.' And turning to Markos he added, 'As for you, take the girl home, do what you like there. Why should we have to watch you making eyes at one another in the square? It's all Margarita's fault, she was out to provoke bloodshed.'

The crowd was taken aback by this unexpected information and fell silent; then everyone started whispering and denigrating Handrinos' daughter.

With this quarrel the Carnival dance at Xacherades broke up for yet another year. Meanwhile night had fallen; the women had gone home; many of the men continued drinking in the wine-stores or singing in the square; Markos had vanished from the scene; but Petros Kladis left on the dance floor with Dimitris said to him, 'Come home with me, this evening I would like to treat you.'

'Whatever you say,' replied Dimitris.

And as they walked along the village main street bidding people goodnight, Petros thought to himself gleefully, 'Margarita, my lass, you'll never marry Markos, and you'll be put to shame as you deserve.' And to Dimitris he said, 'Spy on them, see if you can't expose them.'

'I will,' he replied.

Winter was over and the trees, swollen with new sap and warmed by the spring sun, were returning to life. In the village the peasants were tilling the earth, sowing late seed upon her bosom in the hope that it would take, dressing the vineyards, and returning at night exhausted after the day's toil. In Petros Kladis' household no one ever mentioned Margarita now, or the quarrel during Carnival, and Petros himself seemed to have forgotten all about the insult. Every day he accompanied his hired hands down into the valley and laboured in the fields. But Margarita's life was no longer carefree. Ever since the dance her reputation had been tarnished; the women slandered her and people watched her with suspicion. She was well aware of this, but inwardly she was tormented by an ungovernable passion. She loved Markos with all the ardour of her youthful heart, even if he was only a poor day labourer and she pursued by every prosperous peasant in the village, even if her parents did refuse to let him have her. She saw him frequently and they would tearfully commiserate.

One evening around Annunciation Day* while ascending to the village with her flock she happened upon Markos and turned pale, for as he passed her he murmured softly, 'This evening, at your hut.'

She did not answer and heaved a sigh, pulling her headscarf down over her face in shame; tears started to her eyes and her cheeks flushed red, like the mountain peaks just then irradiated by the setting sun. In a daze she hurried on, while all about her the birds in the trees sang joyously of love's renewal, the grass rippled in the spring breeze that wafted from the vault of heaven, and the fiery disc of the descending sun shed crimson-golden light around as it prepared to plunge into the glittering sea. Nature seemed to swoon as she surrendered to repose and the unknown mysteries of night.

Margarita hastened on; despairingly she brooded over what might come of the passion that had spontaneously sprung up in her heart and so plainly taken root there; she reflected sadly on former times and the loss of her maidenly innocence and tranquillity of soul. And deeply troubled by this invitation from the man who had enslaved her reason and her heart, she made her way along the darkening paths with mounting trepidation. She felt afraid of everyone, suspecting that they were all more or less aware of her illicit longings and watching her maliciously; in her agitated state she feared the very trees and lifeless stones, which to her inflamed imagination might all acquire the gift of speech and bear witness to her heartfelt passion, to the sweet torment of her soul, that everyone considered shameful and grotesque. Involuntarily she clapped her hands to her ears: the little birds were still singing in the trees and she felt convinced that from the verdant darkness they too were condemning her forbidden love.

That night Markos, true to his word, waited for her outside her hut, which was on a densely wooded hillside not far from the village. Soon she appeared, frightened by her own temerity. For a long while after recognizing him in the dark she did not speak to him, nor did he venture to reproach her. All around was infinitely quiet, save for the secret calls of distant night birds, and not a breath was stirring. The lovers surrendered to their desires with all the ardour and abandon of their youth, and the hours of darkness sped away. Through gaps in the bushes surrounding the hut, they could see the waning half-moon slowly ascending, and became sadly conscious that their nightlong amorous adventure must soon end. Then Markos murmured to her, 'My love, the night is almost over. When shall we next meet?'

They both sighed, but as Margarita did not reply he continued, 'Better come home with me. I'll marry you at once.'

'For love of you I'll even do that,' she replied tearfully. 'I've sacrificed everything for you already. But not today, tomorrow — then at least I can collect my clothes.'

The moon had risen higher and a nightingale started warbling its exquisite song. Involuntarily they both listened to it with rapt emotion; how sweet it was, starting very simply, then gradually ascending and becoming more ornate, its vernal hymn extolling nature's reawakening and the desire nestling in every creature, the drive to procreate; on and on it trilled and warbled and made moan and the sound its little throat emitted moved them to the core, making them forget their bodies. Soon the other birds began to sing as well; dawn was approaching and the lovers rose to leave.

But suddenly they heard a laugh outside, an ugly sarcastic laugh that made their blood run cold. Margarita was struck dumb with fear and Markos, stunned, said to her, 'Come home with me, Margarita, if we can get away. We've been found out.' And grabbing hold of her hand, he hastened to the door of the hut.

There was a rustling in the surrounding bushes, as if someone were trying to break through, then someone shouted from very close at hand, 'Out you come, out you come, the pair of you.'

Markos recognized the voice at once; it was Dimitris; he braced himself to fight and defend his Margarita. But just then a man holding a lantern appeared in the gap hastily cut through the thickets opposite the door: it was Margarita's father. He stood there speechless for a moment, his eyes bulging, his face pale with rage and shame, determined to punish them severely. 'God damn the pair of you!' he cursed them hoarsely.

His daughter let out a piercing shriek; but Markos had meanwhile flung the door open and, putting his arm round her waist, ran off with her through the olive grove in the pale light of dawn. From the hut the old man went on cursing them, wanting to give chase. While behind them Dimitris' voice rang out vindictively, 'You've been put to shame!'

By sunrise the whole village had heard with dismay what had occurred that night, and in every shop and home they bad-mouthed Handrinos' daughter. Dimitris himself had taken the first opportunity to break the news to Petros Kladis, who as he listened looked him in the eye, unable to believe at first that the hour of reckoning had tolled so soon. He remained thoughtful for a moment, smiling demonically. Then summoning his womenfolk, who were getting ready to descend into the valley with the livestock, he had Dimitris repeat the whole story, making no attempt to conceal his own delight, and added finally, 'She got what she deserved. But they'll never be able to get married. She's doomed to live in sin forever. Spyros Stratis explained it to me: they had the same godparent at their baptism,* and Spyros is willing to bear witness, as he's a good Christian and fears excommunication.'

Krasades, November 1904

REPUTATION

In the cleft between two steep, densely wooded hills lay a dingle known to the villagers of Skaphidaki* as the Wilderness. But in fact this dell was not a wilderness at all. Its slopes, which fell away quite steeply to the sea, were covered with ancient olive trees, their hollow twisted trunks all gnarled and knotted,* their bi- or tri-furcated branches displaying a myriad of silvery-green leaves that shimmered against the azure of the sky. The ground was strewn with bracken, crushed and yellow after the previous summer and now steadily decaying, ready to give way to the pale green shoots already germinating, which come spring would renew the surface of the earth. Here and there among the thickets, brambles laden with red and purple berries, their thorny runners intertwining, mingled with the sarsaparilla, its fruit dangling like bunches of ripe grapes, while in the clearings wild sage, golden buttercups and stinkweed flourished in the rich soil. Everywhere sheep could be heard bleating, and now and then an ox would low, or a goat scramble up against an olive tree to nibble at the leaves. A little hidden stream flowed down a gully, depositing its waters in the sea.

To this olive grove many women from the village, young and old, would come to graze their sheep and often lingered the whole day. Just then two lasses were sitting at the foot of an olive tree that ivy had locked in its embrace and singing love-songs to a monotonous high-pitched tune. Both were young, about the same age and very pretty. One was Katerina, the other Maria. Katerina was clean, neatly dressed and in new shoes, whereas Maria was barefoot, her skirts torn around the hem and her headscarf dirty; one was from a prosperous family the other very poor. The difference was also reflected in their figures, the prosperous girl being plump, rosy and well-nourished, the poor one lean and scrawny, but with a dark eye that flashed with the vitality of youth.

The sun was approaching its zenith and the girls ended the couplet they were singing, drawing out the last note as long as possible. Maria then said to her companion, 'Shall we move the sheep on?'

'No need,' replied the other. 'There's still plenty of grass around here, but it's getting late so we should eat.' Maria looked down embarrassed and said nothing, but Katerina, sensing the reason for her reticence, quickly added with a sympathetic smile, 'What have you brought?'

'Only bread, and stale at that,' she sighed. 'We're short of everything at home.'

'Same here,' said the other, 'but with cheese and olives. Shall we share?'

'If you like.'

They both untied their napkins and started eating hungrily, making sure they ate at the same pace so as to share the food like sisters.

And as they enjoyed their peaceful meal, Katerina looked about, listening intently. All was quiet save for the distant sound of women's voices, and still further off the crack of a huntsman's gun. She smiled and said, 'D'you think he could have heard us singing all those love-songs?'

'Who?' laughed her companion.

'Who else!' she answered. 'Why pretend? Didn't you admit the other day that Yoryis Vardas is in love with you? When are you getting married?'

'He's ditched me,' Maria said indifferently. 'But I don't care, now someone infinitely better loves me. He has family, houses, everything my heart desires.'

'Lucky you!' replied the other jealously. 'The man I love hasn't started courting me so far. Perhaps he doesn't fancy me, even though his parents raise the matter with my mother every other day. They say I'm the one they want as their daughter-in-law, nobody else! Such a fine young man he is too, there's no one else like him; my heart leaps every time I see him.'

The other girl laughed and her eyes sparkled. 'Well, who is he then?' she asked.

'It's a secret,' replied Katerina, lowering her eyes.

Just then Maria's attention was caught by a spider crawling through the fresh grass. It was a small whitish-yellow creature, with a large triangular abdomen, a tiny head and eight spindly legs. Catching it in her hand she exclaimed delightedly, 'A daddy-longlegs! Now you can consult fate and find out if he really loves you.'

'I'd rather not,' she replied, 'I don't believe in all of that. Ask about yourself.'

'I'll ask about us both. Half the legs will count as yours, the other half as mine. The ones that fall in this direction will be mine.'

Katerina nodded, and smilingly her companion pulled the creature's legs off, letting each one drop. They watched them carefully and both exclaimed at once, 'Look, they're moving, they're moving!' Maria clapped her hands delightedly and added, 'Yes, every single one is moving. So they must be in love with us!'

For a moment they were silent and then Katerina said suspiciously, 'And who's your sweetheart then, Maria? Or are you keeping it a secret too?'

'Not at all!' she replied shaking her head. 'He says he loves me and wants to marry me, so what have I to hide? It's Andonis Mandylas.'

'Andonis?' cried the other, turning pale and clutching her heart, which was beating violently.

'What's got into you?' Maria asked, looking at her companion sharply. 'Is it any of your business, if I marry my Andonis? Are you jealous because he loves me?'

'Me?' replied the other testily. 'Why should I be jealous?' She sighed and lapsed into silence.

'Perhaps you don't like him?'

'He'll never marry you,' she answered, her eyes dim with tears.

'I say he will. Just wait and see!'

'D'you think you'd fit in, joining a well-to-do family like that?'

'I'm a human being, so why shouldn't I?'

'Because it's not you his parents want.'

'Once it's done, it's done. What can they do about it afterwards?'

'Ah, you'll turn their lives upside down!' she replied tartly. 'Anyway, why would he marry you, your father's a pauper? He'll do what's expected of him. He'll marry into a family with property.'

'You're wasting your breath. Like it or not, it's me he loves. He never even turns to look at you.'

Katerina turned pale and angrily replied, 'Nor should he. That would be indecent. You and I are chalk and cheese. He'll cheat you too, just like the other fellow. I'm the one his parents want, like it or not. I'm the one he'll marry.'

REPUTATION

'Wait and see!' she replied laughing with a gesture of contempt. 'Wait and see. I'm the one who'll win him.' And she turned her head away.

But now Katerina resentfully got up and went and sat under another olive tree; her eyes were brimming with tears and she felt sick at heart. Pensively she took out her sewing and continued brooding, when suddenly she heard Maria singing spitefully,

> *Pretty little basil plant, your forty leaves outspreading,*
> *Forty fell in love with you, but I'm the one you're wedding.**

Angrily she responded,

> *Rosy mullet from the sea, my very favourite fish,*
> *I loved you first — but sadly now you're someone else's dish.*

Her rival at once replied more stridently,

> *Though he should climb into the sky and sit upon a cloud,*
> *or hide behind a sunbeam — still 'He's mine!' I'll shout aloud.*

Whereupon Katerina sang defiantly,

> *No threats, no acts of spitefulness will ever wash with me,*
> *Free as a bird am I — and they'll come begging round my tree.*

Her rival however, wishing to bring the altercation to a close, began rounding up her sheep and getting ready to depart. But pride prompted her to sing one last couplet,

> *May all your hopes be dashed, like autumn leaves*
> *Swept from bare branches swaying in the breeze.*

Then she set off. Katerina, determined to have the last word, replied angrily,

> *Don't glare at me and sneak away, like a viper in a ditch,*
> *When it's your breasts they're fondling like any common bitch!*

Maria, who by now was on her way, merely laughed and did not reply, but then, noticing Katerina's mother — a matronly figure with a wrinkled face — approaching, she quickened her step. The old woman lost no time in asking her daughter what the matter was, and then shouted, 'So that shameless slut has come out here to make fun of people! To hell with her, why bother with the crazy madcap?' — But Maria did not hear her, as she was already deep among the shadows of the olive grove, where the leaves were rustling and shimmering in the golden sunlight against the azure of the sky.

Mother and daughter went on discussing the quarrel for some time. Bitterly Katerina explained that Maria was in love with Andonis Mandylas, and this angered and embittered the old woman too. 'Ah, nowadays every beggar is out to make a conquest in some prosperous family,' lamented the old peasant. 'What's the world coming to? But mark my word, Katerina, all she'll reap is shame. I've always said we should give you to Andonis, who is a good and honest lad, and now we've run into this stumbling-block! But everybody in his family wants you, and so they should, as your father is giving you a handsome dowry.'

They carried on like this at length, the old woman's tongue never pausing for a moment. The sun meanwhile was beginning its descent. As they sat there side by side, the daughter finished sewing her new blouse, her mother got on with the family darning and all around the sheep went on grazing peacefully and bleating.

A little later the two women noticed a young man descending the hill opposite, and the mother, who was the first to recognize him, remarked complacently to Katerina, 'It's your Andonis! Look, he's coming our way!'

Katerina bit her headscarf in embarrassment, half hiding her face as she replied in a subdued voice, 'He comes past every day, but I don't believe it's to see me.' And she sighed.

Andonis meanwhile had come up to them. He was a handsome, well-built young man of twenty-two. He greeted the women casually and said, 'I'm working on my property up here during Michaelmas and came by for a drink at the spring.'

'You're welcome,' replied the old woman, and after he had finished drinking she enquired, 'And how are your parents, my boy? It's been days since I've seen them.'

'They're well and send their greetings,' he replied impatiently, gazing about ready to set off again.

But the old woman gave him a sly look and smilingly enquired, 'So when will we be enjoying sweetmeats at your wedding?'

'I don't intend to marry. Marriage is sheer slavery.'

'So you say. You give yourself airs because you're handsome. But I know several girls who are eager to ensnare you. When are you going to commit yourself?'

'You must be joking, Photini,' he replied, bashfully lowering his eyes, 'marriage in times like these, with so much poverty about?'

'Poverty in your family? You're not serious, Andonis. What more could you wish for!' And she gave her daughter a knowing look.

But the young man was getting fretful. He wanted to be off, knowing where Photini's remarks were tending. He gazed about impatiently. The old woman, who read these signs correctly, was annoyed and said, 'Who are you looking for? She left a while ago. Heading for the Pillars.'

'Who?' he asked blushing.

'We know all about it,' she replied. 'Well done, a fine young man like you. And if you marry her, it'll be an act of charity, she is genuinely poor.'

'Who, who?' he asked again impetuously.

'Come now, don't pretend,' said the old woman laughing. 'D'you think you can hoodwink us, who've known you since you first saw the light of day? She was heading for the Pillars, and my guess is she'll be waiting for you.'

'Photini, you talk too much, ' he replied irritably. 'Speculate all you want, but you're mistaken. The Pillars happen to be on my way and now I must be off. Your suspicions won't deter me.' With this he bade them good-night and left.

But the old woman now turned to her daughter, who was sighing with tears in her eyes, and said, 'What cheek, ay, Katerina! It's obvious he's running after her quite shamelessly. No doubt he thought he could pull the wool over our eyes. But they will both be put to shame, just wait and see.'

'Alas,' sighed Katerina, 'she's the one he loves. He goes to meet her every day.' And the tears rolled down her cheeks.

Every evening the village women, married and unmarried, would come to draw water from a large well at the bottom of a hill covered with olive trees and cypresses, in a clearing with a view out over the sea. Beyond the clearing the land fell away steeply, becoming more rocky and uncultivated as it descended precipitously towards the shore. There nature, left unchecked, had proliferated at will, covering the rugged hillside with wild shrubs and flowers. Bushy strawberry-trees* displayed their glories to the sunlight, glossy green leaves, red berries and pinkish blossoms in profusion; beneath every leaf was a cluster of ripening red berries, and beside every cluster a cascade of little blossoms, white translucent goblets fringed with pink; and the green of the foliage, the red of the berries and the pink of the blossoms mingled with the greens of the prickly holly thrusting between them, and the greens of the ground-ivy clinging to their branches, all set against the seared yellows of the bracken that autumn had killed off. And as far as the eye could see the vegetation extended in a blaze of variegated colour, descending to the sandy shoreline rhythmically pounded by the indefatigable foam-flecked breakers of the sea — deep blue, violet, everlasting.

At the well the women were coming and going up and down the pebble-strewn path in little clusters, their empty pitchers balanced sideway on their heads as they descended, and upright, once replenished from the buckets, on the way back, though usually they did not leave at once but lingered round the well to gossip, exchange village news and vent their hopes and their frustrations. Just then some fifteen of them were gathered round the rim listening to one of Katerina's neighbours, an unmarried girl, who was saying, 'I'm told Zopsis' daughter Maria's getting hitched.'

'That's stale news,' replied a young married woman soberly, 'she and Yoryis Vardas have been courting for a while.'

'What, didn't you know,' a slip of a girl piped up, 'she broke off with Yoryis several days ago — or he with her.'

'Really!' exclaimed several voices in surprise.

'Yes, yes,' answered Katerina's neighbour, 'she's not going to marry Yoryis, she's set her sights on Andonis Mandylas.'

'On Andonis,' exclaimed two or three others. 'Holy Mary, she's aiming high!'

One of them then added, 'He too will cheat her. Those Mandylases usually do. They take advantage of poor girls and ditch them when they get bored.'

'As for her, she believes he'll marry her. She trusts him and confides in him. They meet every evening by the Pillars.'

Just then Katerina too appeared. She bade them all good evening and then her neighbour asked her, 'Isn't it true your mother spotted them together?'

'It's true,' she answered bitterly, 'she meets in secret with Andonis Mandylas.'

'Tell us more,' cried several girls at once.

'Alright then,' Katerina sighed. 'Yesterday for no reason Maria bitched at me. She thought I was out to spoil her fun. But why should I care if this or that man fondles her?'

'Wisely spoken, my girl,' a middle-aged woman said approvingly.

'She left Yoryis,' continued Katerina, trying to appear indifferent, 'because Andonis had already caught her eye. She's after the main chance!'

'Of course, of course,' said the neighbour, 'but would the landlord's son ever marry the likes of her?'

'They'd better not misbehave themselves. She's the one who'll suffer if she hasn't the sense to see what she's letting herself in for,' said Katerina gravely.

'She made a proper mess of things with Yoryis,' said another girl.

'It's the same old story,' others observed, shaking their heads.

'Who knows if she'll succeed,' said Katerina. 'Anyway, yesterday she bitched at me and then sneaked off to the Pillars.'

'They'll have prearranged a meeting,' said one lass slyly, a twenty-five-year-old who was always jealous when her contemporaries, especially her juniors, got married.

'Naturally,' replied Katerina, 'and sure enough, Andonis turned up shortly after. But my mother was close by. He asked us for water and then hurried off towards the Pillars. We then gathered our sheep and continued up the hill. My mother, keen to punish Maria for her loose tongue, followed the sound of rustling bracken and found them in a ditch, like bride and groom! . . .'

'Jesus!' they all exclaimed and crossed themselves.

'. . . just as Maria was protesting, "Stop, please don't. How can I get married as soiled goods?" My mother called me across to have a look and true enough, alas, they were embracing... And now they're being lambasted all day long. Not the man, that is, but her...'

'Well I'll be blowed!'

Just then however, Maria herself came down the path to the well, shabbily dressed and dirty but with flashing eyes and looking prettier than usual. Everyone fell silent and stopped what they were doing. She greeted them haughtily and said with a defiant sneer, 'Talking about me, ay? Honest Katerina has told you the latest, I suppose?'

'You've no right to criticize me,' Katerina retorted angrily.

'Ha, ha!' laughed Maria mockingly, 'I'm going to marry Andonis and my enemies can eat their hearts out!'

'Just take care you don't end up walking the streets in town like all the others,' replied Katerina venomously. Then, turning to her companions she said, 'Shall we go then? I don't want to talk to her.'

Several of them swung their twin-handled pitchers onto their heads and set off up the hill with her, looking like an antique procession of libation bearers making their way to some festive rite. The rest followed after them in little clusters, making way for other women descending to fill up at the well.

Maria too left the well and hurried to her parents' house, a dirty unplastered dilapidated hovel in a remote corner of the village. She entered calmly and placed her pitcher on a stone beside the door. Night had fallen and the room was dark and filled with smoke; the flickering fire in the grate gave out a little light. Her parents, seated on a rough-hewn bench beside the hearth, were talking in an undertone, while her two half-naked little brothers were shouting, romping about and rolling on the ground.

'Good evening,' said Maria standing behind her parents and steadying herself against the bed. They did not respond at once and Maria sensed that they were unusually upset and she herself the cause of their distress. She too said nothing and the children suddenly fell silent, without knowing quite why, and, dressed as they were, lay down on the bed.

The fire flared up and a log hissed, emitting a bluish flame; the old woman poked at it and then said gravely, 'Someone's been undermining our good name.'

Old Zopsis coughed and indignantly agreed, 'That's right!' Then without turning his head he addressed his daughter gruffly, 'You're not to go near the Wilderness again and stay away from the Pillars too.'

'What's the matter?' asked Maria timidly.

'You've been misbehaving,' replied her mother.

They all three sighed. The mother got up, came over and looking her in the eyes demanded, 'Tell me, what happened between you and Andonis Mandylas by the Pillars?'

Maria bowed her head and made no reply.

'Did he insult you, either by word or deed?' asked her father, turning and looking at her sharply. 'What did he do to you?'

But even now she did not answer, merely looking meekly first at her father then her mother. The latter shook her head sadly and persisted, 'Something must have happened, because I've been hearing strange rumours too. He's avoiding you and you've been running after him, is that it?'

'Ah, these village landlords,' growled her father angrily, 'they treat us poor peasants like slaves! Isn't it enough that they exploit our labour, claw back our pittance with high interest loans, store-goods on tick and payment for our oil in kind. Do they think they can also affront our reputation?'

The two women heaved a deep sigh. 'Well, in this case,' continued her father poking the fire, 'he is not going to get away with it. Our clan may be poor but it is not dishonourable, and I may be old but I have stout-hearted kinsmen. Out with it, Maria, what did that scoundrel do to you?' He got to his feet. 'Did he make indecent advances?'

'Yes,' replied Maria timidly.

'And you submitted?' cried the mother furiously, picking a stick up from the hearth to beat her daughter with. 'Is that the way I taught you to behave? Is that how you honour us?' she added menacingly.

'It wasn't my fault,' said Maria hiding her face in shame.

'You should have scratched his eyes out,' said her mother.

'He grabbed my hand!'

'Your hand? And you've not said a word since yesterday?'

'Bitch!' old Zopsis cursed her wrathfully.

'You're a disgrace,' screamed her mother, beating her about the head. 'And to think we raised you in our home! But we'll turn you out, or we'll leave you without food or drink and let you starve to death!'

'Did he go further?' asked her father hoarsely, 'did he kiss you, to be blunt?'

There was a momentary pause. The parents stared at their daughter, anxiously awaiting her reply; she looked at them fearfully and nodded.

'How dare you!' fumed the old man, grabbing her by the wrists and shaking her with all his might, 'what d'you mean by bringing shame on me like this?' But then he asked, 'Was anybody else about?'

'Yes,' she replied in a frightened voice, 'Katerina and her mother saw us.'

'Ah, ah, you shameless slut!' hissed her mother and spat in her face, then hit her with the stick.

'So the whole village knows. And you expect to stay under my roof! Get out, get out at once. Either he marries you or you can go to hell.' And with this her father propelled her roughly towards the door and kicked her out.

'Father, mother, Maria,' cried the frightened children, wailing piteously from the bed.

Maria however suffered her abuse in silence; without resisting she slunk away and hid in a corner of the garden, where overwhelmed with shame she burst into tears. She could still hear her father angrily declaring, 'How am I to endure this disgrace?' And his words were accompanied by heart-rending sobs, as if a death in the family had occurred. She could hear her mother beating her breast and cursing her, and realized that she must be tearing her grey hair as well when she exclaimed, 'For every hair I pluck, may a calamity befall her!' Her parents' words seared her vitals and she shook from head to foot with fear.

Again she heard her father's voice declaring, 'Now Andonis has to marry her. My reputation is at stake. So marry her he shall.' Shortly after this she saw the old man come out of the house still muttering 'The bitch, the bitch!' and set off down the hill towards the village.

The long secret hours of the night dragged on, dark and chilly; the wind lashed the bamboo leaves in the garden where Maria was hiding; louring clouds darkened the sky. Intermittently they would be rent by lightning, followed by the deep growl of distant thunder. Maria trembled with fear, shame and the chill night air.

Every now and then someone would come up the road to their house — now a plodding elder, bent by time, now a man in middle life, now a youth with springy step — and Maria would recognize each of them as they opened the door and were caught for a moment in the light coming from within. One might be an uncle, another a first or second cousin. She also noticed that all of them, young and old, came with a gun slung over their shoulder. As each one entered he would quietly greet the company but say nothing more, so that the silence in the room remained undisturbed. Well past midnight her father too returned, accompanied by two more elders.

Shortly afterwards she heard him asking gruffly, 'Well, good kinsmen, have you reached a decision?'

'Yes,' they answered with one voice, and one of her cousins added, 'Either he does the right thing or he must be killed. He shouldn't think because he's rich he can trample on the reputation of the poor! We're an honourable family!'

'May your children and your families prosper,' her mother blessed them. 'Good on you all!'

Then her father's voice, a little calmer now, addressed his wife, 'Lena, go and find the cursèd slut. She can't have gone far. Bring her inside before she catches her death of cold.'

Almost at once Maria saw the door open and her mother emerge half-dressed, dishevelled and exhausted by her grieving and self-laceration. She heard her shout out, 'Hussy, come and let your kinsmen rescue you from shame. Where are you? Come inside!' Timidly she replied, 'I'm here, I'm here,' and hurried towards the house.

As the night drew to a close a man opened the door again and looked up at the sky, which was steadily getting lighter, then went back inside and said, 'It's dawn.'

'Let's be off then,' said the eldest member of the clan.

'Yes, let's get going,' agreed Maria's father. 'Why should we endure an insult to our family a moment longer?' Then he turned to his daughter, whom he had not spoken to since she came in and said, 'You go with my curse. Pack your clothes, all of them, and put on your Sunday best.'

She obeyed without a word, getting dressed in front of the men, who likewise remained silent. The first cock crowed and was answered by the neighbouring cocks, followed by the more distant ones, and then her father said, 'Let's get going then, and may God assist us!'

There were about fifteen of them in all, some in narrow western trousers, others in wide baggy ones, some with straw hats, others with a fez.* When Zopsis gave the signal, they all stood up. The old men went out first, followed by the younger ones, Maria and her father bringing up the rear.

'Good luck,' said the old woman, who remained behind. 'May the Holy Virgin go with you.'

The men were now solemnly descending the hill, swift, silent and determined, their weapons on their shoulders; Maria, with her basket of clothes on her head, was swept along in their midst. Hurrying down the rough path leading from their neighbourhood, they came out onto the main street of the village, and after proceeding a short distance between the slumbering houses, the father stopped and said to his daughter, 'Right, girl, from this point you are on your own, d'you hear? Now go straight up to his house. It will still be locked, but when they open go inside, d'you hear? If they try to throw you out, don't leave. Scream if they beat you but whatever you do don't leave. Better for them to kill you than you leave, d'you understand? Well, off you go.'

Such were his earnest admonitions; meanwhile day had dawned, cocks were crowing from back yards, windows were being flung open here and there, a fine rain was falling and it was cold and wet. Maria stood in the middle of the road irresolute and shivering, while her clansmen waited a little to one side.

'Off you go then,' her father repeated. 'What's done is done.'

She heaved a sigh and, closing her eyes, turned to him and said, 'Give me your blessing, father, I beseech you.'

The old man frowned and shifted his weight uneasily; he looked into her eyes, sensing a hot tear welling in his own. Finally he answered, 'You have it. Go with my blessing, daughter. Only hurry.'

After proceeding on her own for a short distance, she stopped in front of a large well-maintained house in the middle of the village. Her kinsmen stood by expectantly. Soon the door opened unsuspectingly and a middle aged woman, still dishevelled and half dressed, appeared on the threshold.

'Good morning,' said Maria, and before the woman had a chance to block her way, stepped past her with her basket; once inside she added, 'Mother, I've come to find Andonis!' The mistress of the house looked at her haughtily but at first was utterly dumbfounded; then turning white with fury she shouted, 'Get out, you slut, out of my house, you baggage!' And seizing her around the waist she tried to shove her out.

But Maria resisted vigorously and with a sob cried, 'I am staying put, right here, because your son's dishonoured me.'

'What, you bumpkin? So what do you expect? To march straight in as mistress of the house?' Then she yelled out, 'Anastases, come and see what the cat's brought in this morning.'

A tall stout villager in his fifties appeared at the head of the stairs and peered down a moment startled; then flying into a rage he shouted in a thunderous voice, 'What d'you think you're doing in my house? Go back to hell where you belong.' Then he hurried down the stairs, grabbed hold of the girl and managed to drag her to the door. But when he opened it he got a fright. He was immediately confronted by the outraged faces of the entire Zopsis clan, who had tightly surrounded the house and stood barricading the entrance. One of them, a tall handsome fellow in baggy trousers, and the strongest of the younger men, said to him angrily, 'Let the girl stay inside, no one's leaving the house; you are the ones responsible for this and you must put it right. Our reputation is at stake!' And he cocked his gun menacingly.

The landlord became even more alarmed. 'How can you do this?' he protested weakly and closed the door, leaving Maria on the inside; then he hurried back upstairs.

By now virtually the whole village had turned out and the street was packed. From the windows of the adjacent houses women watched the siege with sad frightened faces, waiting to see what would transpire. Voices in the crowd could be heard denouncing landlords who were only too willing to ruin the reputation of the poor, and unanimously commending the actions of the injured parties. Even the chief constable and his deputy were present, but all they could do was look on passively at the noisy milling crowd, which was angrily determined to see the injustice righted, collectively regarding the dishonouring of the poor girl as a public affront. Suddenly all heads turned towards an upstairs window, at which Anastases had appeared, and everyone listened as he announced with trepidation, 'Andonis has left home. What are we supposed to do with her?'

But the villagers below shouted menacingly and shook their fists, while many responded with one voice, 'He's lying, he's lying!' And above the general hubbub, the deep bass of Maria's cousin could be heard announcing, 'We'll burn the house down!* Shame on you, trying to dishonour poor folk!'

At this a clamorous roar arose from every throat and in terror Anastases closed the window. The women at the neighbouring windows beat their breasts and tore their hair, weeping and shouting with the rest of them.

Some time went by like this; then the window reopened and Anastases, livid with fear and rage, reappeared and shouted, 'Our Andonis has done nothing wrong, he did not dishonour her. She was Yoryis Vardas's mistress first. Ask him yourselves. Andonis left her exactly as he found her.'

'All lies and calumny!' shouted several voices and someone fired a shot into the air.

'He must marry her,' roared the villagers, 'yes, yes, he must!'

Anastases closed the window again.

At that very moment Katerina, her face serious, tearful and pale with emotion, her clothes in disarray, broke through the crowd and attempted to enter the besieged house. She pushed open the door, which had not been barred, and in the entrance hall found Maria sitting trembling on the stairs.

'Perverse, wilful creature,' she scolded her. 'See what you're doing? There'll be bloodshed in the village!' Then she proceeded up the stairs.

There everything was in turmoil, Anastases was striding up and down lamenting, his wife was weeping and trembling with fear, while Andonis was sitting glumly in a corner. All three looked up at Katerina and smiled in spite of their distress.

'They'll soon set fire to the place,' Katerina told them gravely. 'Oh, Andonis, how badly you have managed things. They're out to kill you!'

Anastases stopped pacing and looked at her aghast.

'He'll have to marry her,' continued Katerina, 'the crowd is in a frenzy. I've come at a time like this because I respect you, as I once respected your son there. If he'd wanted me he could have had me, but it was not my fate to come and live with you!' And she wept.

Andonis, deeply moved, said to her humbly, 'I feel so awful, Katerina, I didn't know how much you loved me!'

'Now I know what you're like, deceiving innocent girls, I don't want you anyway. God has preserved me!' Then she turned to Anastases and said, 'Call and ask her to come up. Let this be her lucky day.'

'Wisely spoken,' replied Anastases with a sigh. 'He compromised her, now he must accept her.' Then he called out, 'Maria, come upstairs. Your husband awaits you.'

Outside the crowd was in an uproar, getting angrier by the minute.

Timidly Maria came upstairs and looked round for Katerina; then going up to her, she took her hand and kissed it.

'Thank you,' she said, 'thank you with all my heart.'

'Go and sit beside your husband,' Anastases told her, pointing to his son, then he went over to the window and opened it.

The crowd at once fell silent, eager to hear what he would say.

'We accept her. Summon the priest and the best man.'

Immediately the people's rage subsided, everybody started cheering and Maria's kinsmen jubilantly fired their weapons in the air, the church bells started ringing, and amid songs and laughter many people entered Anastases' house.

The landlord greeted them solemnly and made them welcome. And when he caught sight of Maria's father, he shook him by the hand and said, 'It's all God's will. Fetch a bottle of raki and we'll have a drink!'

Krasades, December 1904

HONOURABLE PEOPLE

Dimatsos' tavern served the best wine and some uncommonly fine dishes. It was a spacious flag-stoned wine-store down one of the town's narrow backstreets, dark during the day and at night likewise only dimly lit by a few iron oil-lamps suspended here and there above the tables, the kitchen and the wine-cask spigots. Usually the place was packed, but now it was getting late and most people had already left; only four town tradesmen were still playing cards over their drinks, while two others were deep in conversation, their full glasses before them.

Then an elderly villager entered, a tall man a little stooped with age, a stout stick in his hand. His wrinkled face was not unhandsome for all the ravages of time: his lips were full, his nose broad, his eye still quick and lively. He bade the company good-evening, to which they all responded, then joined the two tradesmen who were chatting, since the lamps above the vacant tables had already been put out.

Then he asked the taverner, 'Could you bring me some food?'

'Fried fish is all that's left,' Dimatsos replied. 'We've been busy this evening. But the wine's immortal.'

'Fine, whatever you have,' said the villager.

The tradesmen eyed the newcomer curiously and one of those not playing cards, an elderly man himself, asked, 'What village are you from, old fellow?'

'From some way off,' replied the stranger, as the taverner saw to his food, 'Ropila.'*

His interlocutor smiled, looking at him quizzically as he sipped his wine; the other tradesman at the table, who from the whitewash on his clothes appeared to be a mason, asked him provokingly, 'I say, old man, have things quietened down in your village, or are they still killing one another?'

The villager's face darkened, he took a sip and then replied, 'Why do you ask about my village in that manner? Don't you know we are honourable people, nowhere more so, even here in town? And there's never any treachery involved, whatever rumours get around.'

'They're an unruly lot, your fellow villagers,' observed the mason with detachment. 'I remember at Ropila years ago we were building a church, Saint Nicholas's I think it was, when an incident occurred that will never be forgotten. It was over twenty years ago now. A certain Glavostathis was killed by someone called Magris.'

The old man looked round at them, sighed, his face assumed a formal expression and he said, 'I am Magris.'

They all stared at him, the four card-players pausing in their game, their curiosity aroused.

'To tell the truth,' said the mason, 'I'd never have recognized you.'

Then Magris launched into his story: 'As I told you, ours is an honourable village, and I am an honourable man. What I did was without guile, as God who watches in the dead of night is my witness. The case is closed now, as I've done my stint in jail. How long? — fourteen years. So why should I deny it? The whole island remembers what occurred, you must be the only one to have forgotten. Do you want to know the whole story from the beginning?

'Old grievances divided us. There had been stand-offs (the fellow, God forgive him, kept taunting members of my gang), quarrels over women, as we were both unmarried, boundary disputes and so on. In short we became sworn enemies and whenever he got the chance he'd do the dirty on me. I patiently suppressed my rage. Then came the municipal elections — since you were building Saint Nicholas's church you may remember them — and of course we found ourselves on opposing sides.

'One evening Glavostathis was sitting in a wine-store with the local councillors. They were calculating how the vote would go. I happened to be passing and overheard them talking about me. "Magris has a sixty vote lead," one of them was saying.

'"I'll fix things so that he never leaves home on the day of the election," replied Glavostathis. I felt insulted, so I went inside and sat down casually among them, as I have here this evening. No one said a word and Glavostathis went a shade paler, as he was in a spot and felt embarrassed.

'The elections came and went. Our victory incensed him and he wanted to get back at me, but didn't quite know how. One day we came across each other on the plain. He was bringing fish up from the sea to market. He glared at me but I approached him, saying, "What's the matter, Glavostathis?"

'"Nothing," he answered without stopping. I followed him all the way to the village, determined to show I was not afraid of him. In the square I knocked his basket over and trampled on the fish. He raised merry hell of course. I paid him for the fish.

'A few days later we again ran into one another one evening at a wine-store in the village. His whole gang was with him, five young hotheads. He leaped to his feet at once and said to me, "Magris, you are dishonourable!"

'I was enraged but I restrained myself — no one should let anger get the better of him — and replied, "Say that again!"

'"You're dishonourable, yes, dishonourable."

'"Say that again!" And he did so, nine times altogether. Then in a hoarse voice I said to him in deadly earnest, "Hold your tongue, Glavostathis. Don't you dare insult me again. If you open your mouth once more, only blood will settle things between us." And I looked him in the eye.

'He glanced around and, emboldened by the presence of his gang, cursed me a tenth time: "You're a dishonourable scoundrel!"

'Outraged by this I answered, "Glavostathis, neither I nor my kinsmen are what you claim. My ancestors and I are renowned for deeds of bravery. Yorgos Skambas, who sealed off that village near the Mills, was from my clan, and I could name a dozen others. Only you, a notorious thief and excommunicant, are what you say. You are the dishonourable one, because I tupped your wife before you. And here are my witnesses to prove it." So saying, I drew a butcher's knife I always carried in my belt and nailed it to the table.

'He turned pale, mortified and shaken by the insult, and flung his fez onto the ground.

'"Draw your weapon," I said.

'"I don't have one," he replied.

'"Go and fetch it then."

'"Where will you be?"

'"Right here."

'Glavostathis was about to leave the wine-store, when one of his wife's relatives offered him his knife. He hesitated for a moment, then grasped it resolutely.

'"Inhuman brute," cried another of the wife's kinsmen, "you're the one promoting bloodshed."

'He made no reply. Glavostathis examined the knife. It was a formidable two-edged weapon. Then he squared off opposite me and waited.

'"Not here," I told him calmly. "Further up the hill, because here they're bound to part us. You leave first and wait for me at Amoutsa. I'll come by there.

'"Right," he replied and left.

'It was late at night, about this hour, and pitch dark. Shortly I set out after him, though everyone attempted to dissuade me. "I'm no coward," I told them. "Two of you come with me. You who gave him the knife and my kinsman here."

'Together the three of us ascended the pebbly footpath. When Glavostathis heard me — even he wouldn't stoop to treacherous ambush — he shouted, "So you've come, ay?"

'"I've come," I replied, halting as I reached level ground.

'Our two kinsmen stood aside. I waited a moment and at once Glavostathis started taunting me: "Why don't you come closer? Getting cold feet? Cursing is all you're good for!" I could hear him approaching. "You're going to pay for everything," he added. Then there he was beside me. In a flash his knife was out.

'"By God, you think you're a brave fellow," I replied, "but to me you're nobody, you're beneath contempt!" I tried to draw my weapon, but it was caught in my belt. Suddenly he lunged at me and stabbed me in the chest. I did not go down though, as his blade had only grazed my breastbone. I took a step back and managed to free my knife, but meanwhile he lunged at me a second time, piercing my windpipe so severely that air whistled from the wound.

'"He's done for me," I thought. But with an effort I managed to control my breathing. Then seizing his blade with my left hand (to this day my fingers are still paralysed — here, look), I swiftly thrust my knife into his stomach. We both collapsed, one beside the other. My weapon had slipped from my grasp as I went down. My ears were buzzing. I saw him get up and was afraid he would finish me off. But groaning like a slaughtered ox he staggered away towards his home. Why? Did he assume that I was dead? Had he lost his knife? Did he scorn to put an end to me?

'I passed out . . . The following evening he expired. I wrestled with death for many days and nights.'

Krasades, March 1905

STALAKTI'S WEDDING

It was the middle of a dark and moonless night; the earth was still radiating heat absorbed from the baking harvest sun during the day; the crickets were chirping incessantly among the olive trees and now and then an owl would hoot. Stathis Plakidas was at home and still awake. Sitting in the doorway of his hut, barefoot and in shirtsleeves, he was smoking patiently and waiting; inside the hut was dark and empty.

'Stathis,' a low voice called out to him.

'Master,' he replied at once, 'good evening, welcome.' He got to his feet immediately, hitching up his baggy trousers. Then kindling some tinder with a flint-stone he lit a taper and with it the lantern hanging by the door, its greasy glass panels blackened with soot.

In its dim light the peasant's appearance could now be made out: he was a tall, thick-set middle-aged man, clean-shaven save for a little grey moustache, and the features of his longish face were ugly.

'Good evening, Stathis,' said his visitor, a handsome young man smartly dressed in western clothes and boater hat. 'Has she come yet?'

'She's husking corn with the other women,' he replied with a sly smile, 'down there on the threshing-floor where you see the light. Listen, you can hear them singing. We've been harvesting all day. Didn't I say you'd not regret placing your confidence in me?'

'We'll see,' said the young man gravely. 'That's what the other fellow said when we began. He ate me out of house and home and now has turned against me.'

'Are you afraid of him?'

'I'm not afraid of anyone but God.'

For a moment they were silent; the young man sat down on a dry log, crossing his legs and leaning back against the fence. Stathis looked at him thoughtfully and said, 'I'll go down to the threshing-floor and let her know. Don't fret if she is late. I'll have to find an excuse to send her up.'

He lowered his eyes, ashamed of what he had said, and set off down the hill through the darkness of the olive grove.

'She'll be mine at last,' the young man said to himself. 'To hell with caution, I've been frustrated long enough.'

Shortly Stathis Plakidas reached the threshing-floor. It was in a level clearing surrounded by young olive trees. A lamp suspended from a branch was smoking; to one side there was a heap of corn cobs, which five women seated on the ground among the husks and beards were shelling with sharp pieces of bamboo, then tossing into a tall pannier. On hearing Stathis' footsteps the women, already worn out by toil and lack of sleep, broke off their song; he approached and trimmed the lamp, which immediately burned brighter; then noticing that the pannier was brim full, he took it under his arm and emptied it out onto the threshing-floor strewn with already cleaned cobs .

'Sleepy, ay?' he asked them as he brought the pannier back. 'Why have you stopped singing? Bear up. I'll let you off early after the dawn shift tomorrow and you can sleep all afternoon. We'll start on the cobs again in the evening.'

'No, not sleepy,' yawned a married woman known as Lena, 'but our throats are parched from gossiping and this evening's meal was peppery. We're thirsty.'

'We've been waiting ages for you to bring us some water, Stathis,' complained his wife Martha, a worthy village matron.

'Too much trouble to come up for it yourself ?' he asked.

'Just following your orders, Sir,' she replied provokingly.

'I didn't think the flask would run out so soon,' he said casually. 'Where's it got to?' The women groped among the husks and soon retrieved it. Stathis, looking at the youngest, a plump girl of eighteen with fine features, said, 'Give my old woman a rest, will you, Stalakti. Fetch us some water from the hut. And remember, the pitcher contains vinegar. The water's in the jug.'

The girl got to her feet at once, unselfconsciously shaking out her dress, took the flask and set off up the hill. She had not gone far when, as if half suspecting something, Martha sighed and sang the following plaintive couplet:

You've built your nest so very high, the bough is sure to break.
And then your little bird will fall, and make your poor heart ache.

The other three women joined her in unison.

'Why d'you sing that?' asked Stathis uneasily.

'Because,' replied one of the girls, 'Stalakti's in love with the best catch in our village.'

'And she'll get cheated,' added Lena gravely.

'Who might that be?' asked Spiros, pretending to be curious

'But it's the talk of the town,' replied Martha to annoy him. 'Tell him girls, or maybe I should — with Master Yoryis Artemes, whose father lives in town.'

Stathis gave her a sidelong glance, but did not upbraid her. Suddenly his attention was caught by the sound of someone in shoes approaching hurriedly. He recognized the figure that emerged into the lamplight at once: it was Yannis Lakouras, a tall strapping young man with fair hair and beard. He gravely bade them good evening and the women welcomed him, eager for his news; then looking at each in turn he asked hesitantly, 'Isn't Stalakti supposed to be working here too?'

'Yes,' they replied in chorus.

'So where is she?' he asked huskily.

'Gone to the hut to fetch water.'

Yannis frowned and looked down fretfully, as if trying to come to a difficult decision, but Stathis at once realized that his questions were not innocent and asked him curtly, 'Is it any of your business?'

'It is indeed,' he answered heaving a sigh. 'It's true, isn't it, you bring the village girls down here to ruin them?'

'Heaven forbid!' exclaimed the three hired women in dismay, as if Yannis were alluding to them personally.

'What d'you mean by slandering our family?' shouted Martha angrily, getting to her feet.

'Artemes' son is at your hut as well. I followed him from the village,' he answered heatedly.

'My God, how shameful, what an outrage!' exclaimed the women beating their breasts and starting to whimper.

But Stathis said to him rudely, 'You're doing this because he dismissed you from his service. You tried to isolate him from the business of the village, so you could act high and mighty using his money. Those days are over. So forget it.'

'I left because I don't like such sordid dealings, but I feel so sorry for that wretched girl.'

'He's not afraid of you, and nor am I.'

'This will not end well. We'll soon see what your new friendship amounts to!' And so saying he set off up the hill.

'Where d'you think you're going?' shouted Stathis. 'My sons will shoot you like a dog. You can't go barging in on people at this hour.' And he whistled loudly.

'Scoundrel,' shouted Yannis over his shoulder. 'Artemes is up there.' And he disappeared into the darkness of the olive grove.

'Alas, what have you done this evening, Stathis,' Martha lamented, weeping like the other women. 'Better to have destroyed a monastery.'

'Oh my God, my God!' wailed the others.

It was daybreak. In Stathis Plakidas' field the five women were harvesting the flaxen corn in gloomy silence; they would cut the cobs one by one from their dry stalks, gathering several into their skirts — held up like sacks with one hand — before going across to empty them into the tall panniers. Then Stathis himself would take the brim-full panniers under his arm, carry them over to the threshing-floor and shake the cobs out onto the heap. But he too worked in silence. And so the cool hours of dawn slipped by.

The sun was already high when Stalakti's father, Thanasis Maravas, turned up at the field, a small shabbily dressed emaciated peasant, bowed down by age and misery. His face was the picture of grief and he hung his head shamefacedly. Stathis hastened over to welcome him and lead him into the shade beside the threshing-floor; he greeted him with a forced smile but the old man said not a word.

'Lakouras must have told him everything,' he thought and waited for the other man to speak first.

The women watched them as they continued harvesting.

'What's this I hear,' Thanasis said after a while without raising his tearful eyes, 'is this what we sent the poor girl to you for? You Judas!'*

'Nothing's happened,' he replied feeling ashamed. 'Pay no attention to the lies you're hearing. Yoryis Artemes came here last night but went no further. Ask the women.'

A glimmer of hope lit up the old man's furrowed brow; at last venturing to raise his head, he looked Stathis in the eye. Unnerved, the latter blushed.

'Judas!' Thanasis said again, going even paler. Then turning towards the women he called his daughter over and she obeyed at once. She too was pale, her lips were dry and her eyes red and swollen.

'He's ruined you,' he told her in despair.

She immediately burst into tears.

'It's not like that at all,' said Stathis eagerly. 'Tell the truth, Stalakti. Your father is hardly going to believe me.'

'He hasn't ruined me, because he loves me,' she replied, wiping her tears with the corner of her headscarf. 'Ever since last year, when we danced together at the feast of Saint Ilias, he has yearned for me, he says. And he intends to marry me, he says, and I believe him. He swore to me, Stathis, with his hand upon your icon of the Virgin, that he'd marry me. Otherwise I'd never have allowed him to embrace me.'

'You did what!' cried her father in anguish, and feeling his legs weaken and his knees give way, he sat down on the ground to prevent himself from falling. Overwhelmed with shame, he hid his face in his hands and wept bitterly.

'Stalakti,' said Stathis after a pause, 'that's not what you told me.'

'Who cares what she told you? It's too late,' replied Thanasis without raising his head. 'All our troubles, all our injustices, come from the rich. Poor folk suffer and the rich behave like tyrants. What am I to do now? And what is to become of her?'

For a moment all three remained silent, then Stathis said anxiously, 'No good crying over spilt milk. Let's see if we can fix things and save her reputation.'

'But how?' asked the old man shaking his head bitterly. 'The girl hasn't a thing in the world. Why did he deprive her of what till yesterday she did have — her honour!' And he started blubbering again.

'Don't carry on like this,' replied the other man compassionately. 'Let's go and find young Master Yoryis and have a word with him.'

'Let's go and hear her sentence from his lips, you mean. She might as well drown herself, poor thing.' And so saying he braced himself and got to his feet.

Just then Stathis' wife approached them and, flinging her headscarf to the ground, cried woefully, 'Alas, we're in deep trouble, Stathis, over this wretched girl.'

Her husband gave her a wry look and set off with the old man.

They ascended the hill to Myrtero, their village, and were now walking along the main street. It was very hot; the sun's scorching rays beat down upon the little whitewashed houses, which in turn radiated back the heat. Not many people were about and only one or two wine-stores were open. But in one of them that belonged to Yerodimos, near the centre of the village, a number of people had assembled. As Stathis and Stalakti's father were passing this establishment, they noticed that inside Yannis Lakouras was holding forth in a loud agitated voice, evidently about the events of the previous night. His tone of voice was angry and accompanied by histrionic gestures, and he would frequently brandish his crook and then hook it back over his wrist. The crowd were listening attentively, nodding their heads approvingly and exchanging glances.

Stathis quickened his pace, tugging the old man by the sleeve; but inside Yannis had already spotted them and, abruptly breaking off his speech, he darted out into the street and stopped them. The people in the wine-store rose in their seats to watch through the windows and the open door.

'So this fox has you in his clutches,' Yannis shouted at Thanasis, grinding his teeth. 'I told you to do one thing, and you go and do another!'

'Watch what you're saying,' Stathis warned him seriously, again tugging the old man by the sleeve.

'So what are you up to now?' retorted Yannis, blocking their path.

'I'm going to make sure things don't get any worse,' sighed Stathis. 'First I'll see if there might be some redress.'

'What redress? Set fire to the big houses! The poor will be far better off.' And as he said this, Yannis brandished his crook menacingly in the direction of a handsome villa on a hilltop surrounded by high walls, above which the tips of lofty cypresses could be seen swaying gently in the breeze.

'I couldn't do that. I'd forfeit my immortal soul as well,' replied Thanasis in a low voice.

'But he deserves it. And then you'd see these procurers starve to death, as they did before Artemes employed them.'

Such were Yannis' words and he was about to continue, when from the depths of the wine-store came the voice of the taverner, a stout serious-minded villager, who shouted out, 'The old man's right. Let him seek some redress for what has happened. What would be achieved by violence?'

The crowd applauded these sentiments and Yannis stood aside, letting the two men continue on their way, then went back inside the wine-store.

Yoryis Artemes was at home, pacing restlessly up and down his spacious living-room, when Stathis entered. 'What's up?' the young man asked him, stopping short at once without formally greeting him.

'The girl's father wants to see you,' he replied much agitated, 'he's downstairs in the courtyard. Promise him what you can, because Yannis is stirring up the village.'

'Have him come up,' said Artemes thoughtfully, and while Stathis went to the window to summon the old man, he said to himself, 'Poor Stalakti, how am I to persuade them to let me marry you?'

'He's coming,' said Stathis, seating himself on a stool.

A moment later the old man appeared; Artemes greeted him with a show of indifference, but received no reply. The wronged father was gazing humbly around the room; he was looking at the furniture, which to him seemed absolutely priceless, mentally comparing this palace with his own humble abode; and he concluded that it was out of the question, given the great social disparity between them, for his daughter ever to be accepted here. His face again assumed an expression of infinite dejection as he gazed intently at the floor.

'Don't you have anything to say, old man?' asked Stathis to break the intolerable silence.

'What can I say?' he replied with head bowed. 'It's up to him to speak, after what he's done.'

Artemes looked at him critically and with compassion, understanding the great bitterness the man must feel, made doubly so by his physical decrepitude and his humiliation; he approached him and motioning towards a seat remarked, 'Perhaps you think I don't love the girl?'

'If you loved her you wouldn't make her wretched,' he replied without moving. 'But God punishes injustice.'

'Don't get angry,' Stathis told him. 'You won't gain anything that way. What is it you want? Speak plainly.'

'Him to marry her,' he answered resolutely, and looked around as if alarmed by his own temerity.

'You're asking the impossible,' replied Stathis gravely.

But Thanasis disregarded him. Pale with uncertainty and grief, he was awaiting Artemes' decision; while he for his part felt the need to placate this man whom he had wronged and somehow satisfy him, and he went on to think about the disturbance in the village, Lakouras' malicious gossip and his beloved's loss of reputation; it even occurred to him that all it would take to defuse the situation was one word from him, which he could always retract later at some opportune moment.

'That is my intention,' he said blushing. 'Will you let me have her?'

The old man's anxious face suddenly lit up, his eyes filled with tears of joy and feeling faint with emotion he sat down. 'Can it be her destiny,' he said after a few moments, 'to become mistress of this house?' And as if he couldn't quite believe it he asked, 'You know though, Master Yoryis, that the girl is very poor?'

'I'm aware of that,' he replied in a subdued voice, as if he felt ashamed.

'And what will your worthy father say?' asked the old man.

'I'll take care of that. He'll understand the situation. But if he's not persuadable we'll resort to other measures.'

Thanasis remained silent for a moment, reflecting that even marriage did not wholly wipe away his daughter's shame, and sighed. 'If you intended to marry her,' he said, 'why didn't you ask me in the first place?'

'What's done cannot be undone,' Stathis told him.

'True enough,' said the old man shaking his head, the tears welling in his eyes.

'I give you my blessing as my son,' he added with emotion. And immediately his sorrow was forgotten, his face became jubilantly happy, his emaciated body felt rejuvenated and he couldn't wait to proclaim Stalakti's unexpected good fortune, this brilliant match, to all the world. 'I'll go and let her know,' he said. 'Oh, how overjoyed she'll be!'

He got up to go; Stathis too rose and followed him out. 'And don't forget,' he told him, 'now you've made such a good match, you must stand the whole village drinks!'

'Yes,' he replied as they departed.

Yoryis Artemes, now alone again, resumed his restless pacing up and down his spacious living-room, pondering the big commitment he had made, and admitted to himself, 'That's not quite what I had intended. Perhaps I was too hasty. A thief is invariably a liar too.'

In Yerodimos' wine-store Yannis Lakouras was still ranting on as furiously as ever. But on seeing the two men return he suddenly fell silent, biting his lip with frustration as he noticed their jubilant expressions. They entered the store and Thanasis sat down formally at one of the tables, saying to the taverner, 'Drinks all round. He's agreed to marry her.'

All those present just stood there marvelling, at a loss for words appropriate to such good fortune, and only Yannis' face went dark. In a hoarse voice he told the old man bitterly, 'He's cheating you. He'll never do it. His parents won't allow it and you'll be left to live with the disgrace, poor fellow. He ought to have been killed.'

'You're talking nonsense, Yannis,' the taverner told him gravely. 'If he's ready to make amends for his mistake, why shouldn't the wedding go ahead?'

'That's right, that's right,' cried everyone and, raising their glasses of raki which Yerodimos had been handing round, they congratulated old Thanasis.

And Stathis, sensing that the villagers were genuinely pleased with Artemes' decision, said to himself, 'Now is the moment for Lakouras to forfeit whatever respect they have for him.' He promptly left the wine-store and hurried off to fetch Artemes from his villa.

Meanwhile the villagers continued drinking merrily, asking Thanasis curiously about the circumstances of his meeting with Artemes, eager to know when the marriage would take place; only Lakouras sat in a corner not uttering a word and when Artemes entered he did not stand up.

The others all welcomed Artemes respectfully, warmly expressing their good wishes. 'Long life!' they cried, as they made room for him. 'Long life to both of you!'.

Artemes ordered wine for everyone and looked round for Lakouras; he caught his hate-filled eye and noticed he was getting up to go. They confronted one another near the entrance; their blood was up.

'Why have you been publicly slandering me all day?' Artemes asked him stoutly.

'Because you deserve it,' he answered angrily. 'Do honourable men behave like this? The sweetest girl in the whole village, and you land her in this situation?'

But on hearing them the people, disinclined to see a quarrel, intervened, while the taverner exclaimed sententiously, 'It's you, Yannis, who are in the wrong this time. Even if Master Yoryis was to blame, he has made amends and, as you see, the girl's father has declared himself well satisfied. Be off then, there's a good fellow.'

'Well said,' cried several voices with approval.

But by now Artemes was incensed and blocked the entrance. 'What right have you to judge me anyway,' he shouted at Yannis, 'when you lived at my expense for all that time?'

'I left because you took advantage of her.'

'That's a lie! I dismissed you because I'm not afraid of you. Your days of laying down the law here in the village are now over.'

Lakouras' eyes blazed, as if he were about to strike him, but Artemes anticipated him and wresting the crook from his hand cried, 'I'll punish you myself, you sponger!' And as he flourished the stick over his head he noticed that no one was leaping to his defence; then suddenly he changed his mind, deciding that it would be better to scorn than strike his enemy, and flung the crook out through the door. 'I won't demean myself. Clear off!' he told him.

The other man went pale; instinctively he reached for his belt, on the point of drawing his knife; but then reason prevailed. 'If I kill him,' he said to himself, 'I shall be sinning against Stalakti, and even though she is already soiled goods, people will say that I destroyed her life.' He heaved a sigh, then looking Artemes in the eye he said, 'This is the first time anyone has insulted me in public,' and left the wine-store looking crestfallen

The fruitful autumn season had come around; Thanasis' family had prepared the wedding trousseau; on every festive occasion Stalakti would wear the costly jewellery the groom had given her; and since they were officially engaged, she was free to visit Artemes without its getting people's backs up. The village no longer seemed to care much and even Lakouras now kept quiet.

On the eve of the feast of the Holy Cross,* in a verdant stretch beside the river, the women were picking the ripe grapes in Artemes' vineyard, singing as they worked. All five harvesters — Stalakti, Martha, Lena and the two other girls — were there again; Stathis Plakidas was supervising the work, helping to load the panniers one by one onto the horses as the women filled them, then dispatching the muleteers to the village with the grapes. The village was some way off however and the road quite rough, so the horses required a good hour to do the round. They had already made four trips since dawn and now the sun was high, its intense beams scorching the green meadows.

'Let's eat,' said Stathis to the women, 'the horses won't be back for a while, as the muleteers will have to feed them in the village over lunch.' And as he said this he strolled to the river and sat down in the shade under a large poplar tree. The women followed and settled on the ground beside him. The river burbled as it flowed along, the silvery leaves rustled in the breeze and birds sang all about. Stathis shared out the yellowish bread, the women took grapes out of their baskets and they all began to eat.

'Just bread,' said Stathis, 'today's a fast day.'

'May we never go without the blessed stuff,' replied Martha promptly.

Stalakti was chewing thoughtfully, as if her heart were not at ease, and after a while she said to Stathis, 'Did you ask the muleteers if he has arrived?'

'He's expected any moment,' he replied and frowned.

'Your father-in-law?' asked Martha with a sigh.

'Yes,' replied Stalakti lowering her eyes, 'we'll see what he says. Ever since we got engaged, he hasn't written to his son. But in any case Yoryis will soon marry me. How could he forsake me now? We've been living together for two months.'

'May all be soon confirmed,' the other women wished her; then Lena added, 'Though they say the old man doesn't want you.'

Stalakti shrugged as if to say 'Who knows,' and Martha sighed and said, 'Poor Stalakti.'

'We don't know anything as yet,' said Stathis gloomily, 'but whatever happens, Stalakti, you are not to blame, it was your destiny.'

No one responded, and they hastily finished off their meal without another word; then the women resumed their work and Stathis sat on in the shade waiting for the horses.

'Today is the day of reckoning,' he reflected. 'Let's see what it brings. There's no chance the old man will agree. The only one I'm worried about is Lakouras. There are storm-clouds brewing.' And with this he stretched out and fell asleep.

He was wakened by someone shaking him and shouting: it was Artemes, who had accompanied the muleteers down to the vineyard on his horse. Stathis leaped to his feet at once, exclaiming, 'What is it, Master?' Then rubbing his eyes with his fists he looked at the young man more critically and noticed he was pale and quite distraught. 'The moment has arrived,' he told himself.

Yoryis meanwhile had begun to explain: 'He came alright. We had an almighty row — curses, shouting and recriminations. Lakouras will be crowing today. But what am I to do? He is my father.'

'And what does he say?'

'I'm to turn her out, or else he'll turn me out. That's why he sent me down here. From now on he doesn't want her to set foot inside our house.'

'You should obey him,' replied Stathis, 'what else can you do? For the time being at least, until he leaves.'

'But he's taking me with him, and he insists we leave tomorrow. He's only staying this evening to give instructions for the vintage.'

'You should obey,' he reiterated. 'You've had your taste of honey.'

'I feel sorry for her though,' he said and tears came to his eyes.

'Time heals all things. This isn't what you intended at the start. But then you got involved. That was not my fault.'

'And am I now to violate my oath? What will the poor girl say to that? And what will people say about me?'

'I don't know what they'll say, but nothing's going to happen before tomorrow. After that God will provide. Anyway, you'll not be leaving her destitute.'

'No. He's agreed to give her land towards her dowry and to let her keep the jewellery. It's just that I can't bear to leave her.' And the tears rolled down his cheeks.

'One does so many things one doesn't want to,' said Plakidas shrugging his broad shoulders. Then he turned towards the women, who were watching the muleteers leaving with the freshly laden horses, and shouted, 'Stalakti, come here a minute.'

She obeyed at once and approached them wiping her face with her headscarf; her eyes looked anxious and her body was trembling and tense. 'Well, here I am,' she said softly.

'The Master has come from the village with bad news,' Plakidas told her staring at the ground. 'We must all submit to our fate.'

'I've heard already,' she replied faintly. 'The muleteers have been discussing it. The old man came. They had a flaming row. And he doesn't want me in their house.'

'And there's no hope he'll change his mind,' said Stathis.

Artemes was in tears throughout all this. 'What am I to do?' he asked her tenderly.

'Whatever your heart dictates,' she answered bitterly. 'Remember you swore on the icon of the Holy Virgin that you'd marry me. Otherwise I'll become an outcast from society.'

'Do you want to come between father and son,' Stathis asked reproachfully. 'Don't you know the young Master has no fortune of his own? What would you live on?'

'I want him to marry me,' she answered plaintively. 'I don't hanker after wealth. I've been used to working like a slave to earn my keep since childhood. I'm sorry he'll be facing hardships too, but that's not my fault. Why should I be made to suffer?'

'You love him, yet would drag him into poverty?'

'Ask him how much I love him. But honour means even more to me than love.'

The three of them fell silent for some time; Artemes closed his eyes while he considered, then sighing he declared resolutely, 'I can't go to war with my own father.'*

'So what's going to happen?' Stalakti asked promptly, alarmed by what he had just said.

'You won't lose out,' Stathis told her. 'They'll let you keep the jewellery and give you land towards your dowry.'

'I don't want their dowry,' she said angrily, 'just the bridal wreath he promised me.'

'Confound it,' cried Artemes, ' don't you see, my hands are tied!'

'I won't let you go,' she replied, flinging down her headscarf and seizing him by the arm in desperation.

'His father is taking him to town tomorrow,' said Stathis in a husky voice.

'So you're renouncing me,' she cried; and slumping to the ground, she buried her face in her hands and sobbed her heart out.

Stathis' good wife Martha now joined them under the shady poplar tree, and looking at the hapless girl compassionately she heaved a sigh and said, 'Poor thing; your marriage has been wrecked, what's to become of you? ... I feel for you as if you were my own daughter.' She wiped away a tear, sat down on the ground beside her wronged fellow villager, who was by now choking with tears, and embraced her warmly. Then, addressing her husband, she added reproachfully, 'Stathis, you've been behind this from the start. I told you that it wasn't right. You're to blame for her disgrace.' And turning to Artemes she pleaded, 'Have pity on her, Master.'

'How can I!' he replied dejectedly.

Stathis now made him a suggestion: 'Let's leave the women to console each other and go and find your father.' And taking him by the arm he gently led him out of the vineyard to where his horse was grazing.

But as soon as Stalakti realized they were leaving, she scrambled to her feet and tearing her dishevelled hair cried out despairingly, 'Where are you going? Don't leave me, how am I to show my face at home?' And a moment later, watching them depart, she again cried out, 'I can't go on living, I just can't.'

'You poor girl,' murmured Martha tearfully, as Artemes mounted his horse.

But then suddenly Stalakti stopped crying; she wiped her face with her headscarf and for a moment stood there motionless, gazing fixedly at the two men as they departed. Her heart urged her to run after them, because instinctively she knew that all would be lost once the man who had wronged her crossed his own threshold without her and shut himself inside; that rejected and abandoned she could neither stay on in her village, despised by everyone, nor find some other refuge, as shame and despair would accompany her everywhere. She also thought of her frail father and his renewed cause for bitterness, and even of Yannis Lakouras who would be forever confronting her and passing judgment.

Almost at once she made up her mind and dashed out of the vineyard after them, shouting, 'Stop, for God's sake, stop.'

But as soon as he heard her, Stathis goaded his master's horse from behind and quickened his own pace, as he too realized immediately that they must reach the house first if they were to avoid scenes before the village crowd that doubtless would assemble. And as he did so he muttered, 'She's running after us, Master. Don't rein in and don't worry about me. I have stout legs.'

The young man did not reply, nor did he look back, but by now the rough road was becoming steep and full of potholes, so that the horse found it hard to get a foothold and kept stumbling and slipping. This slowed them down so much that Stalakti managed to make up considerable ground, still crying out, 'Stop, stop!' The two men could tell from her voice that she was gaining on them and would soon catch up if the steep stretch went on much longer, so they continued to spur on the horse relentlessly. Stalakti attempted to run even faster, despair and her inner tumult giving her unusual strength, and the diminishing gap encouraged her, but she was quickly getting out of breath and could see the men nearing the crest of the steep hill. Once on level ground the horse would gallop off, and then how would she catch up? On and on she ran.

The hillside was covered with cool silvery-green olive trees, and their foliage and the abundant wildflowers partially obscured the road ahead, which now started to curve round; and just at the beginning of the bend a steep and rugged path branched off, rejoining the road higher up and providing a shortcut to the top. Stalakti set off up this path. Panting she scrambled on, conscious of the horse rounding the bend beside her, sweat pouring down her face, her parched throat tormenting her. At last she reached the top, only to see the horse trot past in front of her, while Artemes in the saddle with his back to her didn't so much as turn to look at her. With two or three more bounds the horse crested the hill.

Stalakti felt her strength failing, she could hear her own lungs wheezing and thought she might collapse. She staggered after them, but the horse was now on level ground and rapidly receding. Then she realized that it was all to no avail, that she was being dragged down by fate. At a loss as to what to do, she looked about and noticed a well close by. Suddenly it flashed through her mind that the well would provide a peaceful death and relief from all her sufferings. No sooner had she thought of death than she resolved on it and threw herself in head first. The water seethed from the impact; the walls of the well resounded.

Stathis and the rider both heard the splash and looked round aghast.

'She's fallen in,' cried Artemes, going pale and turning his horse back.

'She's fallen in,' his vassal echoed, his eyes widening.

'We must save her,' yelled Artemes, spurring on his horse as his companion hurried after him on foot.

They quickly reached the well, where the water was still seething, and as Artemes dismounted Stathis leaned over the rim to assess the depth. 'I'm going down,' he said.

'No, I'd never get you out,' replied Artemes. 'Quick, release the saddle-rope and I'll climb down.' As he said this he started stripping off his outer garments, while Stathis rapidly unwound the rope and fastened one end to a nearby tree. Then he ran back to Artemes, now sitting on the rim and tied the other end around his waist. Artemes at once started to climb down, his feet braced against the walls, while above him Stathis held the rope taut, assisting his descent. The well was deep and full of water.

'Stop,' cried Artemes from below, once he had reached the swirling water. He peered about. Stalakti was just resurfacing, her arms thrashing about frantically, and as her head emerged she gasped and spluttered, attempting to cry out, but then the gurgling water closed over her and she began to sink. Clinging to the rope with one hand and keeping his feet braced against the dry-stone walls, he bent down and grabbed the drowning woman by the hair. As he hauled her back up, her hands clutched at his wrist and her nails sank into his flesh.

'Heave,' he shouted, 'she is heavy, I can't pull her out alone.'

'Hang on a minute,' replied Stathis from above, 'someone's coming to lend a hand. He'll be here in a moment.' Then at the top of his lungs he shouted, 'Hurry up, Yannis, they're drowning.'

'Drowning?' cried Yannis Lakouras stunned, as he ran up. Then he added, 'I was on my way down to the vineyard. I knew something would happen, now you've driven her to desperation.' Then he seized the rope.

'Heave,' Stathis told him, bracing himself, 'there are two of them on the other end, heave.'

But Yannis just stood there motionless. Stathis turned and looked him in the eye. Yannis' face was ashen, his eyes protruding from their sockets and there was a cruel expression on his lips that alarmed the older man.

'I'm going to drown them,' Yannis said.

'Heave,' cried Artemes from below, 'the rope's burning my hands like red hot coal.'

'You're what?' exclaimed Stathis, then he saw Yannis draw his knife from his belt.

'He deserves to be punished and why should she live dishonoured?' he replied. 'Was it for this you took her from me?'

Now Stathis shouted, 'Master, leave her and climb out yourself!' and then let go the rope. 'No, no, don't kill him,' he added immediately, hurling himself at Yannis and attempting to disarm him.

'Heave,' cried Artemes again, 'I'm not leaving her.'

Yannis by now was yelling furiously, 'Clear off, you dishonourable pimp, or I'll slit your throat as well.'

But Stathis had lost all fear and, defending the rope with his body, tried to get closer to the other man, until a sudden knife-thrust sent him sprawling wounded to the ground.

Immediately, Yannis cut the rope with his blood-stained knife; the water, churned about by the drowning couple, splashed foaming almost to the rim; the murderer looked round as if appalled by what he had just done.

A crow flew down and perched on the olive tree to which the severed rope was still attached and cawed; raising his eyes Yannis then said, 'I have passed judgment.'

Krasades, June 1905

ILLICIT LOVE

Stathis Therianos, a native of Daphnyla,* was a tall well-built man of forty-four with fair hair and noble features, dressed in western clothes;* he came from an established family and was well respected by his fellow villagers. He lived in the upper part of the village in a modest single-story house partitioned down the middle and surrounded by gardens and pergolas, but he also had a property down in the lower village which he used to store provisions — wine, grain and oil. He was not a proud man and worked his land tirelessly himself, and the earth, tireless in her turn, rewarded his labours generously each year; indeed this season was exceptional, the corn growing abundantly, the vineyards laden with ripening grapes and the olive branches sagging under the weight of their crop.

It was towards noon on a summer's day and Stathis had just returned home from the threshing-floors tired out. He entered the house mopping his brow and called out to his wife, 'Diamando, I'm back.'

Almost at once the mistress of the house appeared, coming up from the kitchen in the basement. She too was about forty but still well preserved, with a generous figure, intelligent eyes and dark hair streaked with gray; she went about the house barefoot, without a headscarf and her sleeves rolled up.

'How is it all going?' she enquired.

'Looks like a bumper crop all round,' he said, sitting down on the bench beside the table covered with a red, white and lilac cloth. 'The grapes look especially promising. I don't think we've ever seen such bounty.'*

'I noticed them too yesterday,' replied Diamando happily. 'Let's hope they ripen. Two years ago they also started well but came to nothing.' And with this she gathered the freshly washed clothes, spread out on the floor for mending, tossed them into a basket and shoved it under the bed with her foot. 'Is our son coming?' she asked after a pause.

'He'd like his meal down in the field. He's still clearing the weeds.'

'Shall we eat then? The food is ready. I was just waiting for you. The girls and the little one have gone down to Phraxolongo with the sheep and took theirs with them. They won't be back till evening.'

'Yes, let's eat,' he replied, shoving his straw hat back and sliding his legs between the table and the bench.

Diamando returned to the kitchen to fetch the meal and Stathis waited, his clasped hands resting on the table. 'How should I broach the matter?' he pondered. 'I'm afraid she won't agree.'

'Don't forget to cross yourself,' she said as she entered carrying a fragrant bowl of peppery bean soup, a yellowish cob of bread under her arm. Then putting the bowl down on the table, she added. 'You begin. I'll fetch the wine.'

Stathis sliced the bread with a pocket-knife he always carried, while Diamando went back down to the kitchen and shortly reappeared with a mug of dry wine mixed with water, which she placed on the table before sitting down beside her husband. Both were hungry and ate eagerly from the same bowl, taking turns to use the spoon and dunking generous chunks of bread into the soup. Neither spoke until they had slaked their hunger. After a pause, Stathis took the mug and raised it to his wife, 'Good health.'

'Good health,' she replied, watching him drink thirstily. 'Let's hope the crops stay healthy too . . .'

'Why anticipate evil like that?' he replied, pushing away his plate.

'But we are evil. Very evil.'

Both lapsed into thoughtful silence for a moment; Stathis wiped his moustache and hands with his napkin and rolled a cigarette; Diamando, having finished her meal and taken a swig of wine, rose to put the leftovers away and feed the crumbs to her hens, a placid expression on her face; then Stathis remarked, 'Every day the household chores seem to be increasing, Diamando. God has blessed our efforts, but we're not getting any younger.'

'We're not dead yet,' she replied with a smile.

'Our son wants to rent a pair of oxen and the harvest is upon us. We'll have to hire outsiders and outsiders will consume our oil . . . so I was thinking . . .'

Diamando looked at him directly, pausing in her task, and for a moment their eyes met. 'What have you in mind?' she asked smiling.

'We should find him a wife,' he replied sighing as if relieved of a great burden and lowering his eyes as if half afraid.

Taken aback, Diamando blinked and frowned, then in a humble tone replied, 'I think you're being too hasty! Haven't you always said you wouldn't think of letting him marry before he was twenty-two? How come you've suddenly changed your mind? And isn't he up for military service next year?'

'But don't many lads marry before that nowadays? Kostas Neroulos, Petros Vlachos, and Yannis Ritsos all married off their sons before they were called up and what harm did it do? Besides, girls don't just wait around, you know.'

'Is that what you're worried about? There's a shortage of men, not women. Don't do it.'

'What if I find him a girl from a good family?'

'No one knows how things will turn out.'

'How does the old saying go? "Marry early, or join a monastery".'*

'It was a different world back then, and there was no military service . . . Besides, he might get bored with her when he returns, more mature and confident.'

'With any other girl he might, but not with the one I have in mind, not if they live a thousand years. She'd bring him quite a decent dowry too.'

'Peasant dowries!' she said scornfully, 'God help us, unless they are hard workers.'

'But she is.'

'Who is this girl you're praising to the skies?'

'Guess,' he replied laughing.

'D'you think I'm blind and unaware! Every time she fetches water or drives her flock past, Stathis, you admire her. Of course I know who you mean, but I'm not happy about it. Our son is still a stripling and she's a buxom lass already.'

'D'you want him to marry some frail ninny who'd infect him with consumption? That's the sort of woman who'd land one with an idiot to educate within a year. But who d'you think I mean?'

'Chrysavyi, the daughter of Aspreas,' she replied without hesitation, adjusting her hair.

'Yes,' he said taken aback. 'Well, isn't she from a good family?'

'Don't do it,' she answered with a shrug.

'Neither you nor I are going to marry her. If our son wants her, he should have her.'

'The lad is still a minor and will do what you say, but you'll be giving him unsound advice. I fear no good can come of such a union. Give him time to toughen up, there's more than one pebble on the beach.'

'Such a girl will never come our way again,' he declared resolutely and got up from the table much displeased; a moment later he added, 'Get his food ready and take it down to him, would you.'

'Of course. But I'll do what I can to prevent this.'

'As you please,' he said casually, 'but it won't make any difference; how can you possibly not like her?'

It was Sunday a fortnight or so later. At Chrysavyi's house, which was on the market square, the Aspreases were preparing an engagement party,* as the match between her and Stathis Therianos' son had been agreed.

Inside, the beds had been removed, the walls freshly whitewashed and a large table set out with refreshments — walnuts, figs, almonds, wine, raki and rum — the sweetmeats divided into separate portions, one for each of the bride's and groom's new relatives.* For the occasion Spyros Aspreas, Chrysavyi's father, had invited all his immediate family, some twenty men and women altogether, who were now awaiting the arrival of their future in-laws and happily discussing Chrysavyi's good fortune. It was still quite early and the bells of the village churches were tolling the end of morning service, when one of the men, who had been watching at the window, shouted, 'Here they come. Here they come.'

Everyone in the house fell silent and Chrysavyi, tall, lithe and buxom and looking ravishing sitting among the other women in her clean dress and scarlet ribbons, went very pale and fixed her gaze upon the entrance to the room. Downstairs laughter and loud merry conversations could be heard, followed moments later by the sound of footsteps coming up, and Spyros Aspreas, a burly middle-aged villager in brand new baggy trousers and *tsarouchia*,* hurried to the head of the stairs to receive his guests, first among them Stathis and his wife. Taking both of them by the hand he led them into the middle of the room, exclaiming, 'May it be a happy and propitious occasion.'

'Amen,' they replied; and while he turned to welcome the rest of their immediate family, also about twenty people, they circulated round the room greeting their new relatives, saying, 'Nice to see you, a match we can all be proud of.'

As the others were responding to these courtesies, Stathis cast an eye round for Chrysavyi, who was looking on with excited curiosity, and went over to her. Suddenly he felt his heart beating unusually fast, a light sweat broke out on his brow, and he tried in vain to think of anything to say to her. 'What can be the matter with me?' he wondered as he gazed at her intently. She was standing shyly and expectantly in front of him with downcast eyes, not daring to move; then Stathis seized both her hands and shook and squeezed them warmly.

Those of the women who noticed remarked to one another, 'How fond of her her father-in-law is,' and waited to see if he would kiss her. But Stathis seated himself on a bench and drew Chrysavyi down beside him, saying, 'I've long had a soft spot for you, Chrysavyi. I'm so delighted with the match! I feel you'll revitalize my family.'

'I shall do my best to love your son,' she replied without raising her eyes, 'and I shall obey you and your wife as if you were my natural parents.'

Stathis kissed her brow with a little thrill of pleasure, whereupon Chrysavyi rose to greet her mother-in-law, kissing her on both cheeks, then proceeded to shake hands with all her new relatives as they came forward one by one. Then holding hands with Diamando, who seemed extremely happy, she again sat down next to Stathis.

Stathis had now become preoccupied and seemed oblivious to what was going on around him; he kept stealing glances at the future bride and felt perturbed as he took in her youthful charm and the beauty of her face and figure, but he told himself he should be proud of such a daughter-in-law joining his family, the prettiest girl in all the village. Yet for all that, his heart could not rejoice.

'Why?' he wondered. And from deep within a warm glow suffused his whole being. Suddenly he realized that he himself desired her. Immediately his hairs stood on end and his conscience rebuked him, telling him that this unfortunate notion infecting his reason was utterly absurd, and he said to himself, 'I feel ashamed.' Indeed he actually blushed for shame. How could such an illicit idea have ever entered his head? His blood began to seethe insanely, his face and hands felt hot and he became afraid that someone might notice his agitation and divine its cause. Anxiously he cast his eyes around the room, then smiled with relief on seeing everyone heedlessly enjoying themselves; only his wife looked at him a little quizzically, but even she smiled back, evidently delighted with the warm reception from the in-laws. Unconsciously he clasped Chrysavyi's hand and felt a pang of anguish in his heart; immediately he let it go, stood up hastily and went over to the window.

'Hot, eh!' he remarked to the first person that approached.

'It's the crowd in here,' the other laughed; then both fell silent.

He leaned against the windowsill facing the room and despite himself kept turning the matter over in his mind. 'Get thee behind me, Satan!' he told himself. 'It's sinful to be even thinking of such things, she's going to be my daughter!' He tried to laugh it off, telling himself that what he felt was just innocent paternal love, or would become so, since he knew that all he could expect from her was sweet friendship and affection, like the love his children bore him. 'I'm not a child,' he concluded, 'unaware of what I'm doing.'

Meanwhile Chrysavyi's father was ushering his guests over to the table, asking them their preferences and pouring them their drinks, and having made sure that everyone was comfortable, he sat down next to Stathis for a confidential word, while the others carried on vociferously talking.

'When do you want to have the wedding?' he asked him.

'Before the vintage,' Stathis replied after a moment's hesitation.

'I've no problem with that,' the other said, 'but they must not wear rings, so the groom doesn't keep coming round. A point of principle with me. Well, let's drink their health.'

They clinked glasses and as he sipped his wine Stathis overheard Diamando saying to the bride-to-be, 'You'll have your jewellery within the week. What do you prefer, broaches or pendants and gold chains?'

'Whatever you decide,' replied Chrysavyi.

Stathis, eager to please her, put down his glass and said, 'She deserves the very best and she shall have it. I want her to have lots of trinkets. The jewellery will be here by Sunday and she'll go to church adorned with gold.'

'What a lucky girl,' exclaimed several women, overhearing Stathis' remarks.

Then Spyros Aspreas raised his brimming wineglass and shouted jubilantly, 'Good luck to them, may their union be a happy one. May they have their mothers' and my blessing. May they live to see their grandchildren. And may you all, my worthy in-laws, live long and prosperous lives!'

'And here's to the marriage of all your other children,' they shouted with one voice as he downed his glass; then one by one they began sipping their drinks and nibbling the sweetmeats, everybody laughing and conversing merrily, praising the two families that were being united, envying Chrysavyi her good fortune and even singing nuptial songs.

Midday was approaching and things were still in full swing. From the street came the sound of many voices carolling a *mandinada.** Another party down below was singing as if in response to the songs of the company upstairs. Everyone could make out the words of the lead singer:

> *Pretty little basil plant, your forty leaves outspreading,*
> *Forty fell in love with you, but I'm the one you're wedding.*

'It's the groom,' cried the bride's mother. 'He's serenading you, Chrysavyi.' And tears came to her eyes.

Immediately everyone crowded to the windows. Down below five or six young men, clustered round the groom — a tall handsome well-dressed youth as yet with no moustache — were warbling the couplet one last time, drawing out the final note melodiously as they gazed up at the windows.

The bride-to-be appeared holding Diamando's hand and the groom greeted her from below with a smile and a little wave. Bashfully she covered her pretty face with the corner of her headscarf.

The two months had passed, it was the beginning of October and once again a Sunday. Ever since dawn gun shots and church bells had been incessantly resounding in Daphnyla to announce Chrysavyi's marriage, and the whole village had turned out to admire the pretty bride and enjoy the rare spectacle. After the service, Stathis' family set out from the upper village, the violins and muskets leading the way, followed by the priest, the groom and the best man; everyone was dressed to the nines for the occasion, the men immaculately clad, some in western suits others in rustic baggy trousers, the women decked out in their finery, gold trinkets adorning their bosoms, ears, throats and wrists, all smiling and in happy festive mood. The violins played, the muskets boomed and the whole assembled clan marched swiftly through the village square and stopped outside Aspreas' house.

As soon as they were seen the door was opened wide, allowing those out on the street to see inside the house, and many voices exclaimed admiringly, 'Look, the bride, the bride!'

And sure enough, Chrysavyi was slowly coming down the stairs holding her mother's hand, and everybody watched as she paused on the third step and looked back for one last glimpse of the beloved home* where she had been born and rocked in her cradle, and then wiping away a tear proceeded on down the stairs, her mother still beside her. When she reached the bottom, one of her brothers, the eldest, who though a year or two younger was about her height, embraced her round the knees, lifted her over the threshold and placed her on a large stone which stood outside the house against the wall.

'Ah!' exclaimed everyone in rapt amazement.

The bride stood motionless on her elevated perch with eyes downcast, her features radiant with emotion and tears rolling down her blushing cheeks, her resplendent costume sparkling. Her bosom was covered with gold trinkets, broaches, chains, buttons, stars and crosses, almost concealing the spotless white linen of her tight bodice which so enhanced the lovely contours of her figure while leaving bare her neck, adorned with bands of fine-spun gold and rich red coral. On her head she wore a spotless white silk headscarf, artfully folded back to show off her face; her hair was braided with fine tasselled cords, dressed with broad white muslin streamers, and tied high up around her head with many-coloured ribbons.* Over her bodice she wore a short purple velvet jacket embroidered with gold thread, complemented by a deep blue shot-silk dress cascading in rich folds down to her ankles; her fingers were adorned with rings of every kind.

Everyone was awe-struck and kept exclaiming to each other, 'What a costume!' 'What a bride!' 'The village hasn't seen a wedding like this for years!'

Stathis went pale as he gazed at her, 'What a gorgeous woman my son is marrying!' he said to himself and felt utterly dejected.

Over the past two months his obsession with her had grown stronger, because he saw her every day; and every day he admired her more and his heart rejoiced to see her. He had quickly realized that he lacked the strength of will to part with her, but he had stubbornly kept all sinful thoughts at bay and tried to persuade himself that his passion was natural and pure, and thus he let it conquer him. And now he was captivated by the radiance of her beauty, by the bashful way she gazed down at the ground, and he brooded bitterly over the fact that it was his son who was to marry her. Involuntarily he compared himself and his own child and judged his son the lesser man. 'Why should it be him?' he asked. And at once, as if frightened by his own reflections, he said to himself, 'Where's the Tempter leading me! Is my flesh capable of resisting such abominations?' He turned pale with anxiety, but no one noticed, as all eyes were gazing at the bride, whom his son was just offering a helping hand down from the stone, before linking the little finger of his right hand with the little finger of her left. And that same moment the troubled Stathis heard the muskets boom and the violins strike up, saw the bride and groom set off, flanked by the priest and the best man, and felt himself being urged from behind to follow them. Fearful lest anyone should notice the turbulence within his soul, he started out after them absorbed in thought.

While the priest was conducting the marriage service, Stathis remembered his wife's words and regretted not having heeded her advice. Standing in his pew* he reflected that in a year his son would be off on military service and his bride would remain at home without her husband. What torment if he managed to conquer his desires, but what a frightful curse upon his family, upon the entire village, upon Christianity itself, if the Tempter were to triumph! Involuntarily he started at the thought. 'That will never happen,' he told himself and tried to laugh it off. But his face remained grim.

'Is something wrong?' asked Diamando, who was standing in the pew beside him, and she touched his hand.

His blood froze. 'I'm fine,' he replied hastily. 'I was overcome with joy.'

After that he tried to focus on what the priest was saying as he rapidly read out the blessings, only raising his voice for the responses. But he couldn't concentrate; he stared fixedly at the bridal couple standing motionless before the altar, the groom crowned with a golden wreath, the bride with one of silver, each holding a candle, and he could not suppress his grief. It occurred to him that there was still time to remedy matters if he were to halt the proceedings. He closed his eyes and tried to imagine how this might be done, but his mind boggled and he dismissed the succession of ideas that came to him as out of the question. He started listening to what the priest was saying, and suddenly realizing that in a moment the best man would exchange the wreaths and their union would be eternal and indissoluble, he tottered; he must do something right away; he wanted to cry out loud in protest; then as if waking from a nightmare he opened his eyes and looked around him fearfully; his gaze fell first on the bridal couple then on the relatives standing looking on with radiant faces, and he realized how ridiculous his resolve had been. What would they do if he were to shame them for no apparent reason? Nervously he clenched his hands and cracked his knuckles. 'What am I to do, what am I to do?' he murmured under his breath, and as he realized that only death could now release him from his conflicting passions, he yearned for and cried out for it; and raising his eyes to the holy icons in tearful supplication he murmured, 'Mercy, mercy!'

Meanwhile the sacred rites continued in the time-honoured manner; the priest bore witness to the couple's mutual vows and the best man exchanged the wreaths, at which Stathis, unable any longer to control himself, groaned aloud and feeling faint sat down in the pew to prevent himself from falling.

'The incense must have affected you,' said Diamando, putting a hand on his shoulder. But he did not hear a word and, nonplussed, she gave a little shrug . . .

On recovering he realized that the exchange of wreaths was over and the bride and groom now seated, and he noticed the in-laws going up to kiss the wreaths. He remembered that he himself was supposed to do this too, and summoning all his strength he got to his feet.

As he approached the bridal couple he hesitated a moment, then kissed his son on the cheeks and wreath, and as he kissed the bride's wreath he said to her trembling, 'You are now my daughter and I shall love you with all my heart.'

His face was ashen and his son asked him with concern, 'What's the matter, Father? Are you not feeling well?'

'Joy,' he replied hoarsely with tears in his eyes. 'Joy like grief deprives one of one's reason.' Then he reflected sadly, 'Whatever now happens is my fate.'

The nuptial banquet was a memorable event. All the relatives ate, drank, laughed, became intoxicated and caroused. And in the afternoon a splendid dance got underway in the main square of Daphnyla and continued until sunset, after which everyone returned to the Therianoses' house for supper. This meal too was lavish but the guests, still sated from their midday feasting, ate in moderation; the men did full justice to the wine however, repeatedly raising their glasses to the bride, the groom and the best man. After supper the singing began, and after that the in-laws proposed dancing the *syrto** inside the house.

No sooner had dancing been proposed than the younger men leaped to their feet and started clearing the tables, chairs and benches out of the way, making the women too stand up; and once the room was ready everyone joined hands and formed a circle. Only the elderly remained seated, the men sipping their wine in one corner, the women chatting in another.

Stathis too had joined in the *syrto*, his face radiant with happiness as he took the bride by one hand, she extending her other to the groom. The dance was now ready to begin; a woman known for her fine voice began a lengthy song and everyone, men and women, sang along with her as they stepped out with their right foot to the rhythm of the music. At first their steps were short, slow and sedate, but as the tempo of the song increased the dance became more lively and expressive; sometimes the circle would contract as everyone moved towards the centre and then expand again; sometimes the dancers would step sideways or make little leaps, especially at the end of each progression. The women smiled happily as they sang, their bodies, heads and hands all moving gracefully, while the men sprang lithely in the air, criss-crossing their legs to display their mastery of the various figures. Stathis held the bride's hand firmly, encouraging her to leap higher as he watched admiringly, and she, carried away by the euphoria of the dance, sang with abandon, her voice soaring above the others, her jewellery jingling on her breast, her face flushed and sweating. The groom too watched her with desire, but Stathis even more so, indeed such was his self-knowledge that he had completely forgotten all his earlier soul-searching and wished only that the rapture of that dance might never end. But now the song drew to a close, the dance concluded with a climactic leap and everybody laughed with delight. They let go their hands, mopped their brows and started to disperse.

The old men continued drinking in their corner, the elderly women went on quietly gossiping in theirs, and two or three other women who had not joined in the dance began another shorter song.

Then Chrysavyi's father made his way into the centre of the room, where a few people were still lingering, and announced, 'What about dancing the *fourlana*!'*

'I'll lead off with the bride,' cried Stathis, taking her by the hand again.

'Whatever you say,' she replied.

'And I'll dance with you, Amalia,' said the groom, turning to one of his cousins.

'Count us in,' shouted a third couple.

'Let's have the violin!' cried Stathis enthusiastically.

'But it's the groom who should dance with the bride first,' protested Diamando, just then appearing among them and giving him a severe look. 'That's the customary order.'

'Never mind,' replied Stathis embarrassed. 'She's dancing with me now. I'm her father, aren't I?'

They said no more and the violin struck up a brisk lively melody.

'A change of tune,' remarked the worthies sitting over their wine.

The men took up their positions opposite the women, their heads cocked a little, their lips smiling. Then they clapped their hands and the women raised their skirts, their eyes downcast. Whereupon the couples stepped out to the rhythm of the music, advancing and retreating to left and right, placing their hands on their hips, twirling them behind their heads, swinging their arms from side to side, their faces and bodies in animated motion; and still in time to the music, the men would prance and strut towards the women pretending to embrace them; but the women would deliberately evade them, turning their backs, escaping to one side, or flouncing past them; then the same pantomime would begin again, the men making as if to catch the women, the women pleading with expressive gestures, feigning shame or joy or grief or terror as they leaped and whirled about, clutching their breasts and looking round or tossing back their heads; and as the violin played the same tune ever faster the dance accelerated, until finally as it approached the end each male seized his partner by both hands and together they spun round and round, thunderously stamping out the last crescendo. The dance was a representation of the triumph of love. Then Stathis, warm and impetuous from dancing, embraced the bride ardently and kissed her on the forehead before letting go her hands.

Red in the face and sweating, she pushed him away a little and looked him directly in the eyes, then shyly half-concealed her face behind her headscarf.

Diamando, who again just happened to be close by, remarked to her husband with a reproachful look, 'That's not part of the dance!'

'As soon as I recover,' said the bride, 'I'll dance with my husband too.'

'He's in love with my daughter, Diamando,' said Chrysavyi's father teasingly. 'Don't be jealous now.'

Everyone who overheard this laughed; Stathis said nothing and withdrew to a corner of the room, mechanically wiping his brow. Spyros came across to him.

'For all your forty-five years,' he said, 'you dance as well as the best of the young lads.'

Stathis smiled absently and made no reply; he filled his glass with wine and, while the bridal couple were preparing to dance a second *syrto* and the lead singer was rehearsing another song, his expression darkened and he said to himself, 'You're getting carried away. Don't overstep the mark!'

Just then the light from the lamps grew dim.

'Top up the oil,' said Spyros. 'Or perhaps it's time we left the newly-weds alone?'

'No, no,' replied Stathis anxiously and his heart contracted. 'Ah, if only time would stand still,' he reflected with a sigh, and he hastily got up and refilled and trimmed the lamps.

Then he returned to his seat, relieved to find that his brother-in-law was no longer there, and as he sipped his wine he thought to himself, 'Soon everyone will be leaving. And Chrysavyi? What am I to do?' And as if he were two different people, the voice of Conscience replied, 'But isn't their union natural, proper, human, God-ordained? What do you expect? Didn't you yourself arrange it all?' 'But I want her myself,' he said pathetically, and shuddered. He cast an eye around the room, fearful lest anyone had heard the unseemly words his heart was uttering, but the guests were all dancing and revelling unsuspectingly, and he hid his face in his hands. 'Even in Sodom they did no worse,' he said to himself, 'yet God sent down fire upon them! It's sinful even to be thinking of such things!' He shook his head trying to dismiss these thoughts and poured himself another glass of wine. But then his eye was caught by the slender figure of the bride, who just then was leaping in the air enchantingly, her face all smiles, and the turmoil in his heart increased and tortured him. He felt like weeping. 'Soon everyone will be leaving,' he thought, 'and then what will become of me? How can I prevent it? Ah, woe and misery!' And the other voice replied, 'Prevent what? Their blessed union for the sake of your damnable lust? You have the shameless audacity to drag the hapless creature entering your home into the mud? Steer clear of it, such thoughts are utterly dishonourable!' 'Dishonourable, yes,' he admitted with a groan, 'but how am I to act? For two months now I've been burning in the fires of hell, the Tempter's on my back and I am doomed.' And a moment later he decided, 'I think I shall get drunk.'

The *syrto* had come to an end, several couples were getting ready to dance another *fourlana* and Stathis noticed the bridal pair among them. He felt his heart contract and got up to go, without quite knowing where. But just then he noticed Diamando beside him and sat down again, embarrassed.

'What's the matter, are you feeling ill?' she asked him with a smile.

He shook his head and Diamando continued, 'All the relatives are looking at you. A wedding celebration in your home and you behave like this? What are people going to make of it? Pull yourself together!'

He got up without a word, too besotted to respond; then noticing that the bridal couple had resumed their seats, he relaxed a little and going over to the other corner joined the old men who, by now quite tipsy, were laughing without reason and drinking to excess.

'What a party you've put on tonight,' one of them remarked to him.

He made no reply and envying their merriment, settled down to drink.

It was past midnight and one by one or in family groups the relatives were leaving. Stathis' brain was now befuddled, but the wine had not extinguished his desire. Suddenly he felt himself seething with hatred, envy and malice and realized that his frustrated yearnings were driving him to commit an outrage and the wine fortifying the inclinations of his heart. His eyes were bleary and his face had gone quite pale. As he anxiously watched the guests diminishing, he felt compelled to do something and rage getting the better of him he started singing bawdy songs at the top of his voice, stamping his feet in an attempt to let off steam. But when they heard him the relatives just laughed and continued on their way, while Diamando put out the lights without a word. 'He'll soon fall asleep,' she told herself and sent the bridal couple off to bed.

Stathis' blood was seething, but suddenly a glimmer of reason penetrated his inebriated mind and he stood up with a shudder; some obscure instinct for self-preservation propelled him towards the door and out of the house. After wandering here and there he took the valley road towards his hut, still warmed and dizzy from the wine; he found the night air pleasantly refreshing and was reluctant to go home. But beneath the first few olive trees he stumbled over a hollow log and fell, and so feeble was his willpower that he made no attempt to rise, merely rolling over onto his back. In the dim nocturnal light he could see the trees whirling round him, intermingling and changing places, he thought the earth was moving and when he closed his eyes he felt as if he might be falling. He did his best to keep them open, but then he fancied he could see frenzied snakes with glowing eyes and monstrous quadrupeds lurking among the shadows of the dancing olive trees; and to his feverish imagination every beast was a human being transformed, a sinner whom God's justice had condemned to a feral existence in the woods; he even thought he could hear these grotesque creatures howling and moaning piteously as they licked at female corpses, trying to revive their former paramours.

Amid these oppressive hallucinations he fell asleep, but his slumbers too were turbulent and restless . . .

He was wakened by the chill air of dawn. Sober now, he felt bewildered, not recognizing where he was, but slowly it all came back to him and he got to his feet at once. His head was aching and felt muzzy. His first thought was not to return home but to emigrate, no matter where, far away from sinful temptation. He made his way towards his hut. The sun was rising and the leaves of the trees glistened with tiny drops of dew, while the early morning air was fragrant with the scent of autumn flowers. By the time he reached the hut it had occurred to him that he would not be able to leave that day, because at home the nuptial celebrations would be continuing in the customary way and his absence would give rise to gossip; it gratified his wounded heart to have discovered this impediment. 'I'll leave some other day,' he told himself and set out on the road back to the village.

Crossing the square he ran into many of his acquaintances, all of whom congratulated him, and he was obliged to shake hands left and right, buy drinks for several of them in the wine-store and listen to them sing the praises of the bride and groom, which made him jealous. He noticed however that everyone spoke to him cordially and thought to himself, 'How different they would be if they could see into my black heart.'

Soon he arrived back home again; his wife was cleaning and tidying the living-room, which was still upside down after yesterday's festivities.

'Good morning,' she said looking at him anxiously as she approached him. 'You got drunk yesterday, where have you been all night?'

'At the hut,' he replied warily. 'Bandits take advantage of these celebrations.'

'You could have told me before leaving. I waited up all night.'

'Did Yoryis do so too?'

'Oh no, he and the bride went to bed. I didn't want to disturb them on their first night together.'

'Ah,' he cried out, turning pale.

'What's the matter?' she asked looking him in the eyes, 'God preserve us, you're not sick?'

'I'm alright,' he replied, a forced smile on his pallid lips.

Diamando shook her head sadly, then as if intuiting his thoughts, asked spontaneously, 'Are you displeased with our son's marriage? Isn't it all natural enough?'

'Why should I be?' he replied. 'Didn't I arrange it?'

'Then why with the wedding celebrations in your house do you behave as if it were a wake? Aren't you embarrassed? What will people say?'

Not knowing what to reply, he shrugged his shoulders and then asked, 'Have you seen them yet?'

'They're just getting up, can't you hear them?'

Stathis sat down on the doorstep and Diamando brought him his coffee, then briskly began tidying the house again. After a while the bedroom window opened and Stathis watched as his son happily and proudly looked up at the sky to gauge what time it was, and then he watched the bride approach him and put her arms around him.

'Oh God,' he groaned in anguish, covering his face.

'You're jealous,' exclaimed his wife from inside, going pale and trembling. 'They did no worse in Sodom. The village will go under for your sin. Shame on you!'

He looked at her dumbfounded.

'Men go mad three times in life,' she continued, 'in youth, in middle age and in their dotage. May God forgive your sinful thoughts, because you're clearly not in your right mind.'

'But how am I to . . .' he began.

'Just pull yourself together,' she replied, giving him a contemptuous look. But they did not have time to discuss things further, as gunshots rang out close by, followed shortly by footsteps and loud voices. It was the relatives returning for the second day of celebrations and, as was the custom, they were bringing bread and chickens for the festive meals.

October had come and gone; the newly-weds were enjoying life, Diamando was vigilantly watching her husband's every move and Stathis, aware of his wife's suspicions, did his utmost to conceal his passion; but from the day of the wedding he was a changed man, consumed by jealousy and racked by conscience and to console himself he turned to gambling and drink. The family was threatened with a major catastrophe and Diamando realized that she must make every sacrifice to avert the danger.

One day she found herself alone in the house with her son — her daughter-in-law and her other children had gone off to gather olives and Stathis had descended to the wine-store — and she said to him gently, 'Yoryis, my son, you have my blessing. May you be happy with your wife. But you must also realize that your father and I are not getting any younger. Soon you'll be having children and for us that will mean a lot of extra bother. Besides, I'm a difficult woman and don't like two mistresses under the same roof.'

'What are you saying, mother?' he answered, tears starting to his eyes. 'Have you suddenly become hard-hearted?'

'I have other children to consider,' she continued gravely, despite herself, 'and they are female and more vulnerable.'

'So what?'

'I have to look after them as well . . .' Then, as if displeased with the direction the conversation was taking, she added in a coarser tone, 'Let's not beat about the bush! I want us to live separately!'

'Live separately? Am I in a position to set up on my own and support the wife you've given me? Why have me get married?'

'He'll let you have some land.'

'I'll go and see him right away,' he replied, deeply hurt.

'Wait, it's nearly midday and they'll all be back for lunch.'

No sooner had she said this than Chrysavyi appeared at the door.

'In fact we're here already,' she said smiling. Then noticing that they both looked tense she added gently, 'What's the matter?'

Diamando gave her a sidelong glance and adjusting her headscarf replied curtly, 'We're going to live separately. Your father-in-law will let you have the other house and some land to live off. I intend to remain the mistress of this house.'

'And so you should,' Chrysavyi replied offended, 'but why split up?'

'Because I'm difficult!'

'But we've never quarrelled.'

'Well, we are about to.'

'Mother, don't,' pleaded Yoryis.

'Be quiet, boy,' said Diamando, 'Chrysavyi does just as she pleases in this house and I won't have it.'

'What have I done then?' she asked tearfully.

'Without asking me you gave the beggar bread. My comb is missing. So's my soap. What's happened to them?'

'Have you brought me here to crucify me?' she replied dejectedly. 'At home I used to receive better treatment.'

'That's why we should live separately.'

'Don't be unkind, Mother,' Yoryis begged again. 'Don't scold her. She's not done anything.'

'That's enough from you, young whippersnapper. When your father gets back, we'll sort the whole thing out.'

With this Diamando descended to the kitchen, leaving them in some distress. After a while Stathis appeared, a cheerful expression on his face that morning. But on entering the house and seeing his son and daughter-in-law disconsolate, he realized something had happened and asked them anxiously, 'What's up?'

'She wants to turn us out of the house,' replied Yoryis in a loud voice.

'Perhaps she thinks it's hers,' said Stathis flushing, 'that she brought it to me with her dowry?'

'What cheek,' shouted Diamando hurrying back upstairs and, flinging her headscarf on the table, she continued, 'You have the face to talk like that? I could whip you!'

'But he's right,' said Yoryis looking at his father and expecting him to respond in the same aggressive tone.

But instead Stathis sat down on the bench and started whistling, as if he didn't give fig; Diamando thought to herself, 'Poor girl, I feel sorry for her, but it can't be helped, I must prevent worse from happening.'

Chrysavyi was by now in tears and Yoryis said, 'Mother, you'll drive her away, why can't you behave like a mother?'

'Because I'm old and crotchety. You must set up on your own.'

'But why have me get married? You both said the family was short of hands at harvest time!'

'I was against it. Your father is to blame,' said Diamando. 'Let's not make the quarrel any worse.'

'Why must you upset her?' said Stathis anxiously.

'You're the reason why!' replied his wife.

'Father is a kind man!' sighed Yoryis.

'A plague on all such kindness!' she replied angrily. 'But I've told you I'm perverse and I want to live in peace!'

'You must be out of your mind!' said Stathis.

Yoryis looked at her amazed. Never before had he seen her speak so sharply to his father, how could he put up with it without losing his temper?

'All this fuss over a crust of bread!' said Chrysavyi plaintively.

'And where's she to go in a month or two when I'm called up?' objected Yoryis.

'God will provide,' Diamando said resolutely, 'but now I want you out!'

'Pay no attention to her,' cried Stathis raising his voice. 'She's not in her right mind.'

'Every day there will be endless quarrelling like this,' shouted Diamando. 'I want to be mistress in my own house.'

'What if I leave you?' said Stathis ominously.

'Don't you threaten me!' she replied, raising her finger.

'Holy Mary, what a family!' cried Chrysavyi, seeing that things were getting rough. 'I don't want to live with you any more either. As I've caused so much disruption, we'll go our own way. Or better still, I'll go back to my father so as not to deprive you of your son.'

'Ah no, I don't want that,' said Diamando. 'As the Gospel says, "those whom God hath joined together let no man put asunder".'

But Stathis, seeing his daughter-in-law upset like this, became deeply distressed himself and his eyes too filled with tears. Quite unconscious of what he was doing, he went over to the girl and embraced her, cradling her head and murmuring 'Don't cry. Don't cry,' then kissing her on the forehead several times. So sweet did touching her feel that now he couldn't bring himself to let her go; a warm wave suffused his whole body and oblivious of all else he tried to kiss her on the mouth.

'I don't believe it!' cried Diamando indignantly and gave her husband a violent shove.

'Let him comfort her,' said Yoryis, 'you see how you've upset her!'

But Chrysavyi was alarmed; she sensed that her father-in-law's caresses were unnatural and repressed and suddenly suspecting his sinful urges, her blood seethed with resentment. She raised her eyes and looked searchingly at Stathis and with a shudder recognized his perverse desires; then she hid her face in her hands and cried, 'What place is this I've come to!' And when Stathis approached her again, she pushed him away before he could touch her, then told her husband, 'Yoryis, either we move out this minute or I'm leaving!' And pale and trembling with rage she glared fiercely at her father-in-law.

Stathis hung his head, his heart pounding against his chest; conscience reproached him and, regretting that he had dared to sully the girl's purity of heart, he said impulsively, 'I too can see it, we're just not going to get along. Move out to the other house. I'll let you have some land. Go with my blessing.'

But even as he said this he felt himself bristling with resentment; he was filled with searing hatred as he reflected ruefully that he was at that moment sacrificing everything he most desired, and recognized that such a sacrifice was quite beyond his powers. Greatly perturbed he got to his feet and in a daze went out into the road.

Diamando now returned to the kitchen and with tears in her eyes said to herself, 'I behaved harshly, but it was the eleventh hour.'

Upstairs the young couple prepared to leave the house.

Things appeared to have settled down. Yoryis and his wife were living in the house lower down the village, Diamando had made sure they were allotted fields not bordering on the ones they retained themselves, so that the two households were not neighbours either, and all winter there had been plenty of work, each family harvesting and pressing its own olive crop, which that year seemed never ending.

Could Virtue be prevailing within Stathis' heart? This was what Diamando asked herself and hoped, since after the split her husband had returned to normal; he attended to his tasks, had stopped playing cards and drinking, kept regular hours and never lost his temper.

But the change was far from genuine and within him his passion was seething unendurably, indeed it had intensified because it was repressed; nor did his conscience reproach him any longer and all his psychic energy was directed toward one goal, that of satisfying his lust. Now however, even though jealousy tormented him a great deal, his mind was lucid. He was no longer carried away by passion. He had seen how his lack of self-control had betrayed him prematurely and brought about the separation, how it had opened his wife's eyes and needlessly created suspicion in the woman he desired so much; in short it had jeopardized the success of his objective because one was now watching like a hawk, the other on her guard. Stathis had realized that only cunning stratagems and subterfuge would enable him to deceive the two women, indeed he would need great patience to regain their confidence. And once this Satanic thought had taken possession of his mind, he assumed a mask. He behaved as if his soul were serene and innocent, as if he harboured no other sentiment towards the girl besides good will, indeed so skilful was the hypocrite in his dissembling that with time Diamando's opinion gradually began to waver and the good woman asked herself whether he had really come to his senses and escaped the slippery slope toward illicit love, or whether he might not have been blameless in the first place and his behaviour simply the effect of the wine and his unbounded happiness. 'How could a passion so reckless as to contemplate a crime subside so quickly?' she asked herself. 'How come he no longer sought out his daughter-in-law, how come his emotional turmoil had not increased since the separation?' And she concluded that the danger must have passed.

The bride was having much the same thoughts. Alarmed at first by her father-in-law's strange conduct and made suspicious by Diamando's sudden angry outburst, she herself had insisted that they part; she recalled his sparkling eyes, his fond caresses and his fiery kisses, but who could tell whether his intentions were malicious, whether he really had a villain's heart. She feared she might have suspected him unjustly; from the beginning he had shown her great solicitude, and in giving his son so generous a portion when they moved out he had proved how much he had their interests at heart; so perhaps his love might have been innocent, no different from the affection all fathers have for a son's wife. Perhaps happiness and the wine had both affected him; but since then she could not fault his conduct; she had not received one suggestive word, unseemly glance or hint of impropriety from him, rather in his unstinting cheerfulness, courtesy and frankness he showed that he wished her to be happy with her husband; and so day by day Chrysavyi's fears diminished and her father-in-law rose in her esteem. If Yoryis did not have to leave, they might go on living amicably like this for ever, but she was apprehensive about the time when her husband would be away.

Stathis was well aware of what the two women were thinking and felt inwardly elated. 'Patience,' he said. 'My son will soon be gone. He who bides his time will not go hungry.' And this hope helped assuage the torment of his jealousy.

It was now May, the harvesting was well advanced and young men who had turned twenty-one and were eligible for military service, Yoryis among them, were preparing to draw lots. One day while this was in progress Stathis said to his wife casually over supper, 'Our son is making progress, Diamando. He's worked hard and made a profit. Yoryis is like me . . . when it comes to husbandry.'

'How much better off we'd be,' she remarked, 'had we not divided the property.'

'You were the one who wanted it,' he replied with a shrug.

'You were behaving so strangely.'

'Really? Well, you know what wine can do. And now we're all at peace.'

'The snag is, Yoryis's number may come up,' she said ruefully.

'Then we'll just have to take Chrysavyi back,' he answered smiling.

Diamando did not reply and looked at him searchingly for quite some time.

Autumn had come round again and the day of Yoryis' departure was approaching. It was afternoon and Diamando was standing in her doorway spinning, her back against the marble doorpost, an apprehensive expression on her face. When she saw her son approaching the house with his father-in-law, she pursed her lips wryly. Stathis was not at home.

'Good afternoon, sister-in-law,' cried Spyros. 'Hello, Mother,' said her son.

'Welcome to you both,' she replied, 'but I'm afraid Stathis isn't here.'

'It's you we've come to see,' said the older man, 'shall we go inside.'

'As you wish,' she said, moving aside to let them enter then following them in. Once inside she seated them at the table with its striped tablecloth, put aside her distaff, served them wine from an earthenware jug and stood waiting to hear what they had to say.

'Our whole clan was sorry when you split up.'

'Why? It's given us all more peace of mind. My son knows what's his and we know what's ours. Isn't that always the way it happens when one's children get married?'

'Ah, Mother,' sighed Yoryis, 'you were more fond of me when I was single.'

'I'm still very fond of you,' she replied with a look of deep affection.

'I've been called up, Mother. Where am I to house her?'

'With her family,' she replied, stealing a glance at Spyros.

'You mean here,' said the father-in-law testily. 'She has no other home.'

'We don't get on.'

'She will obey you. You'll have no cause for complaint while your son's away, I can assure you.'

And not receiving an answer promptly he added, 'I don't want people laughing at us — and laugh they will if I take her back when her husband has parents in the village.'

'What if she were to live on her own?' said Diamando quietly, without really believing such a thing could ever happen.

'On her own, so young,' exclaimed Yoryis. 'I won't have it. I'd rather emigrate with her for good.'

Diamando thought to herself, 'God help us if Stathis decides to bring shame on us while the lad's away. And if she is living on her own it will be worse. As her father-in-law he will have the right to come and go. And would I be able to keep an eye on them the whole time?' A moment later it occurred to her that she could confide her suspicions, not of course to her son for fear of turning him against his father, but privately to Spyros; but then again she reflected that the way things looked at present, these suspicions seemed quite groundless, so how could she defame her husband?

'Well?' they asked her.

'We'll see what my husband thinks.' She said this because it struck her that if her husband felt his heart might weaken, he would be only too pleased to overcome his illicit passion and avoid perdition by refusing to accept her. But both men replied together, 'He wants her.'

At this, not knowing how to refuse, yet still reluctant to say yes, she replied with a bitter smile, 'Ah, so you've agreed already.' But then immediately, clutching at one last hope which suddenly flashed through her mind, she added, 'I'll talk it over with my daughter-in-law. We still have time enough.'

'Just as you like,' they replied delighted. Then they turned to discussing other matters, the wine which was poor and scarce that year, the weather that made it hard to till the land, the local news, and finally military service. Diamando urged her son to come back to the village now and then, if not to please his parents and siblings then for the sake of his sweet wife; she exhorted him to behave and be obedient lest he be punished and his return delayed, and she gave him her blessing. Then she thanked them for their visit and as the sun was setting the two men rose and left, happily waving her good-bye. Taking up her distaff again, Diamando resumed her place in the doorway; as darkness fell dark thoughts kept coursing through her mind and scarcely moving her lips she murmured anxiously, 'I fear we'll become the village laughing stock. May God's hand protect us!'

The next day Diamando happened to meet her daughter-in-law at the well and they greeted one another; Chrysavyi, who was paying no attention to the gossip and laughter of the other women, was about to swing her pitcher onto her head.

'Fill mine up, will you,' Diamando said smiling as she placed her pitcher on the rim. And while her daughter-in-law plunged the bucket into the well she added, 'I want a word with you, Chrysavyi.'

The other woman looked at her without replying and when the pitcher was full they set off towards the village, steadying their burdens with one hand.

'Do you want to come to us when your husband leaves?' she asked her unexpectedly.

'They want me to,' she replied at once, giving her a sidelong glance. Diamando, as if reading her thoughts, stopped short and said, 'I know the situation!'

'What d'you know?' she replied blushing.

'My husband . . .'

'I did suspect it,' Chrysavyi interrupted her embarrassed, 'but might I not have been mistaken?'

Diamando shrugged her shoulders. 'Does your husband know anything about this?' she asked.

'Who'd have the heart to tell him? Then they'd be at daggers drawn.'

'Absolutely! . . . But do you want Daphnyla to become another Sodom?'

'Me?' she protested, going pale.

'Keep your voice down, people might hear us,' she said quietly and added, 'What's to be done?'

'What's to be done? My family don't want me back.'

'What if they hear about this?'

'Would they ever believe it? The thing's so unnatural. They'll say you've made it up because you don't want me in your house.'

'I'm afraid for my children! The girls are vulnerable, who will marry them if their father gets an evil reputation?'

'Don't think about such things, don't insult me. You know I'm innocent.'

'I mention it for your own good,' said Diamando looking at her fondly. 'May God preserve us.'

For a few minutes they walked on thoughtfully in silence, then Diamando continued, wanting to frighten Chrysavyi, 'I know my husband — he's fiery and irascible, and when his blood is up he can't control himself. He's kind-hearted, but all his kindness can vanish in a moment. At present he is docile, but who knows how he'll behave over the year. Ah God, I would have married someone else, but he took me by surprise and brought me home with him. Accursed be the evil hour! But for that, we'd not be in this situation.'

'Mother, I tell you nothing's going to happen. I'm an honest girl with honourable parents. I was brought up strictly by my own mother. Besides, our suspicions may be mistaken. For a whole year now I've had no reason to complain about him.'

'Have you seen him in the last day or two?'

'Yes, today. Your son brought him over!'

'And what did he say?'

'He seemed afraid of you and will leave it up to you.'

'God have mercy on us!' she exclaimed and said no more.

They were now approaching the outskirts of the village and passed a housewife on her way to the well, her empty pitcher on her shoulder.

They greeted her and she stopped to have a word.

'May you be safe from the evil eye,'* she said. 'You look more like sisters than mother and daughter-in-law. And it's good to see you going about together, pleasing to both man and God.'

'Nice of you to say so,' they replied.

'Quarrels occur in every family,' said the stranger, but how does the old saying go?

> *A man and his wife may quarrel and brothers may go wild,*
> *But a mother and her daughter are quickly reconciled.'*

'But we haven't quarrelled,' they replied.

'And of course, you'll be living together now your son is off? . . . Naturally, what else?'

'Yes,' they replied with one voice and said good-bye. Once they were alone, they looked at one another surreptitiously and sighed; both realized that they would be doing what society expected.

Yoryis had departed and Chrysavyi was living with her in-laws; for two whole months nothing had disturbed the family's tranquillity, and neither woman had any complaints regarding Stathis' conduct.

Chrysavyi was always serious in his presence and barely said a word to him, quietly going about her chores in and around the house; and to maintain a becoming air of sadness in the absence of her husband, and avoid giving her father-in-law the slightest pretext, she never wore her trinkets, rarely changed her white bodices, even soiling them with smoke, and avoided wearing scarlet altogether, plaiting her hair with green and white ribbons and wearing her sash inside out tied up with yellow tape.

Diamando was pleased with the modesty of her demeanour, but her mind was not at ease. She feared her husband's apparent indifference might be feigned since, alert to his every move, she noticed how he was always cracking jokes and his laughter seemed quite forced, how his eyes would sometimes sparkle or glaze over, especially when he thought he was alone, and how his sleep was often fitful and he would awake in fright, as if terrified by his own imaginings. She did not admit her fears however, and at home took every opportunity to talk of Yoryis, praising him, counselling her daughter-in-law to be patient, and urging her to write to him. 'The months will fly,' she told her. 'Two have passed already. He'll soon be back and we'll all be joyfully embracing him again, especially you, my dear.' She even mentioned — usually in Stathis' presence — that Yoryis might show up unexpectedly if granted leave, and whenever the young man wrote, she made Stathis read the letter out several times to them — neither woman had much formal education* — until she knew it virtually by heart; then she would discuss it with her, leavening it with her own advice. But even when no letters came, Diamando would often admonish her daughter-in-law in an earnest gentle voice. She was the one who talked the most when the family assembled for a meal or sat round the kitchen hearth on cold winter evenings. She never tired of uttering honest pieties and instructing her daughter-in-law on how to be a good housewife, help her family prosper and keep her husband happy. She would dwell on the dangers every woman had to overcome, especially if young and reasonably pretty, because to men, she said, a woman is merely a commodity, bought today and sold on to someone else tomorrow. Occasionally she would try to provoke her husband, referring to God's compassion in sending last year's bounteous harvest, and predicting many more, provided people kept to the straight and narrow and did not incur His wrath, especially with the kind of sins now often heard of on the island, where dissolute conduct was on the increase and honest, God-fearing judges dedicated to cracking down on crime long gone. For the most part, Stathis would listen to her with smiling indifference, but occasionally his face would darken. Then Diamando would renew her assault more blatantly, citing examples of this or that person who had stooped to illicit relations with his sister-in-law or cousin, violating God's command and the laws of nature and religion. Her words would scald him and upset him, and he would blush and change the subject awkwardly, and the more Diamando witnessed his confusion, the more she would needle him by dwelling on the wages of sin and the sinner's sorry end, despised by everyone even if he were wealthy and a village elder. Such a man would find no peace even in death, she claimed, the earth would not dissolve his body and he would become a vampire, frightening good Christians and eternally accursed. In this way the good woman hoped to keep her husband's conscience alive and preserve her family. But she did not confine herself to words alone; all her efforts were concentrated on preventing the crime. She didn't mind if the household chores were neglected, provided she could stay close to her daughter-in-law or leave her children with her, giving them prior instructions not to leave her on her own, especially if her husband were around. And on the rare occasions when her daughter-in-law had to be left alone, Diamando made sure that Stathis did not know about it.

He however was daily sliding further down the slippery slope. Satisfying his lust had become the primary object of his life and all his mental energy went into trying to evade his wife's surveillance. Through unflagging observation of the women's habits, he was able to guess when his daughter-in-law would be alone in the fields for a short time, and one day — it was by now February — he found her at work in the little garden beside the hut. His mind was made up.

On catching sight of him the girl panicked. She instantly sensed that all was lost and tried to get away. But he grabbed her round the waist. His eyes were bulging, his nostrils quivered and his heart was pounding violently. She started struggling and screaming, but he clamped his free hand savagely over her mouth and dragged her forcibly into the hut.

Summoning all her strength, Chrysavyi managed to prise his hand from her mouth and at the top of her lungs cried out, 'Remember I'm your daughter-in-law!' and went on shrieking frantically, but by now her strength was flagging.

Stathis kicked the door shut and sent her sprawling to the ground.

'Dear God, dear God,' she wailed amid floods of tears, 'don't rage against your people, visit all your wrath upon my head!' And then she fainted.

But from that point on she would wallow in the mire of sin.

It was on the evening of Maundy Monday — that year Easter fell on the twenty-third of April — the church bells had rung for vespers and Diamando and Chrysavyi were getting ready to attend the service, having sent the children on ahead with their father.

But before they could leave the house, Stathis returned in a state of agitation and announced, 'I've just received a letter; he'll be home for Easter.'

'What a welcome surprise!' Diamando immediately exclaimed, looking at her daughter-in-law and husband with delight. But

Chrysavyi, she noticed, didn't say a word and her eyes wandered despondently around the room before coming to rest on Stathis, who hastily turned his back on the two women and pretended to be looking for something by the bed.

'Aren't you both pleased?' cried Diamando, suddenly suspicious.

'Is he really coming?' asked Chrysavyi biting her headscarf.

'Don't tell me a curse has come upon my home and children!' cried Diamando, wiping away a tear.

'Keep your voice down,' Stathis begged her desperately. 'In God's name, in the name of Holy Week, don't let people hear us.'

'Bitch,' Diamando continued furiously, 'what hell will accept your sinful body? Even Satan will refuse you... And you, shameless father of our children, and old enough to be a grandfather, what have you done!... Did you not fear God's fire, excommunication by the Church and the abomination of the village?'

With this she started wailing inconsolably; Chrysavyi stared at her in terror, while Stathis, who had sat down on the bed in shock, listened with anguish to her imprecations; but reason told him he must make her hold her tongue at once, if the villagers were not to hear them.

'Steady on, steady on,' he said in a thick voice, 'you're condemning me unjustly.'

'Your voice betrays you,' she answered passionately. 'How could you bring such shame upon your family and me, whom the women will all point at when they find out... and find out they will because, by Christ's wounds, God never lets such crimes remain a secret, he exposes them to punish us.'

'Don't shout, Mother,' Chrysavyi also begged her in a faint voice.

'I'm not your mother,' she replied furiously. 'A fine Easter we'll be celebrating, a fine Christian family, ours! And you were preparing to enter the house of God like a pair of excommunicated rats? Weren't you afraid an earthquake might bring down the church upon you and all those innocent Christians perish because of you?'

And Stathis, stung by her rebuke, replied heatedly, 'Stop shouting such outrageous lies! You're being misled by false suspicions. And if Yoryis should get wind of them from others and turn vengeful, I might end up on the gallows, because, mark my word, I won't let him kill me!'

'Alas! Alas!' wailed Chrysavyi. 'A curse upon my fate!'

'I know,' said Diamando giving him a contemptuous look, 'that you're capable of anything, abominable man! Cursed be the hour she first set foot in here! May Christ have mercy on his sinful world!'

For a few moments all three fell silent. The blackened lamp hanging in a corner spluttered and went dim, not a sound could be heard outside and Stathis sat there motionless, trying to collect his thoughts. Suddenly Diamando's heart was lightened by a ray of hope: 'Perhaps they were not yet guilty, perhaps God had intervened in the nick of time to prevent this most grievous of sins.' Then she thought with anguish of her son's bitterness, were he some day to hear of his unprecedented dishonour, and raising her hand she said, 'Swear to me, by Christ's suffering and this hallowed Easter-tide, did you or didn't you commit this crime?'

Stathis heard these words with the elation of the castaway who sees a piece of timber from the wreckage of his ship, and getting to his feet buoyed up by hope, said in a stout voice that belied the trepidation of his soul, 'As God is my judge and my defender, nothing happened. You are tormenting us with your unwarranted suspicions. Have pity on her.'

Chrysavyi stared at him aghast; Diamando, a bitter-sweet smile mingling with her tears, now looked at her and said, 'Now you too swear!'

The girl had no time to consider and with a shudder resolved to perjure herself as well, knowing that this would end the matter, but her own words betrayed her. 'This cross-examining is suffocating me,' she cried, 'I was a human being and for the last three months now . . . have become a beast. How has my flesh endured such sinfulness! And now how am I to face your son?'

Diamando clapped her hands to her ears in horror and a wave of fury swept through her; she looked round for some weapon, intending to take justice into her own hands, but then reason prevailed. 'Am I going to take her sins upon myself,' she reflected, and a chill ran down her spine. But feeling compelled to do something, she shouted out, 'Incestuous monster, perjurer!' Then seizing Chrysavyi by the hair, she shook her violently, flung her to the ground, spat on her, then spat in her husband's face and, not knowing what else to do, rushed out of the house screaming, 'This is the house of Sodom. Christ has been re-crucified this year by you. Far better to have destroyed the

monasteries.'
Eventually she found her way to the church.

Absorbed in contrite prayer, Diamando did not hear the chanting, the priest's litanies, or the whispers of the other women, who eyed her curiously, trying to fathom the secret of her ardour, nor did she notice the congregation, the sacred icons and the candles, utterly absorbed as she was in seeking guidance from Him who rules the universe and the destiny of man. Her honest conscience showed her the right course to take. Her family must not become a laughing stock; God who had allowed the Tempter to triumph would favour her by keeping their shame a secret and not punishing her innocent children or herself; let his wrath fall upon the guilty, let the godless miscreants suffer whatever they were destined to, let them pay for their atrocious sin. She herself must stop taunting and cursing them, she must be patient and behave with dignity, she must placate God with daily prayers, fasting and contrition, she must appeal to His compassion. And her son who would soon be home must not hear anything, not a word; God would give her the strength to conceal her devastation, to suffer alone and smile. In the end God would be merciful and raise the incestuous couple out of the mire.

Such were her prayers; but when she had entered the church the service was already almost over, and now she noticed people stirring, heard the priest invoking the saints' names and giving the final blessing, and she crossed herself. She too moved forward and bowed before the icons and as she kissed them felt the tumult in her soul subsiding. Then she looked round for her children and they all set off home together...

They found the door open, but inside all was dark. They could hear Stathis' voice: 'Let's go,' he was urging, 'or there will be another row.'

'I just can't move,' replied Chrysavyi tearfully.

'They're coming,' they heard him saying in a husky voice.

'What's happening?' asked Diamando's eldest daughter on the verge of tears.

'Go in through the kitchen,' Diamando replied, 'go to bed, my angels, lest what you hear corrupt you too.' And with a sigh she crossed the threshold, lit a lamp and looked around. Chrysavyi was still sitting on the floor, her hair dishevelled, her eyes puffed up with weeping, and Stathis was standing over her pale and distraught, his straw hat on his head and a thick staff in his hand, as if about to set out on a journey, while beside him lay a bundle of clothes wrapped in a sheet. When they saw the look of alarm on Diamando's face they both fell silent, but then the children outside began to wail, 'Father! Chrysavyi!' and tried to enter.

Diamando however barred their way. 'Off to bed with you,' she repeated severely. 'Go and sleep in the kitchen as I told you. You too are becoming disobedient far too young. What d'you mean by howling in the street?'

They obeyed at once. Then Stathis told Chrysavyi, 'Come, let's go, you can hear her getting angry.'

'Where will you take me? Am I to live with you in sin forever?'

'Your husband will be here on Sunday.'

'Kill me so I don't have to look people in the eye!'

'He's the one who'll kill you. She's bound to tell him. But he won't get me.'

'I don't want his to be the hand that slays me. I don't want him to go to hell. You take on the guilt — finish me off.'

But now Stathis grabbed her wrists impatiently and pulled her to her feet, then putting the bundle of clothes under his arm he shoved her towards the door.

'Think of our children,' cried Diamando, who up till now had been staring at them in stunned silence.

'Father! Chrysavyi!' wailed the children from the kitchen.

'Where do you intend to go, accursed couple?' Diamando then asked, lowering her gaze.

'We'll go where fate leads us' replied Stathis. 'It's hard for anyone to bear such shame.'

'But then people will give us the evil eye at Easter,' cried Diamando. 'I suppose you don't care what people say behind your backs.'

'One way or another they'll curse us. Best not to have to listen.'

'If you stay, no one will ever hear anything about it! What am I to tell our son if he doesn't find you here?'

'Really?' said Stathis smiling hopefully, but then as if suspecting Diamando might be laying a trap for him he added darkly, 'I'm not so easy to snare, if you're thinking of betraying me.'

'As if I were like you!' she retorted, turning her head away contemptuously, 'I'm doing this to prevent the gossip, to prevent our son's being devastated over Easter and disaster following.'

'But he'll want to sleep with me,' wailed Chrysavyi.

'Pretend you're ill,' replied Diamando, recognizing the sinful implications with a shudder.

'Everything that's happened to me was my destiny,' cried the other woman faintly.

'It's your two heads that are to blame,' said Diamando with a deep sigh.

'I'll have to sleep with him,' Chrysavyi added, 'I'll just have to, otherwise there will be bloodshed.'

Diamando looked at her, trying to guess what she might have in mind, then turning pale she shook her head sadly. 'You're mocking both man and God!' she declared and tearfully descended to the kitchen to avoid sleeping with her husband. Her children gathered round her weeping and she embraced them all and kissed them on the forehead, murmuring, 'Poor things, poor things. Evil has indeed befallen us this Easter.'

Yoryis had come and gone without suspecting anything, nor had the village got wind of anything amiss. Time rolled on; Diamando no longer paid any attention to Stathis or her daughter-in-law; she avoided their company, didn't speak to them or prepare their meals, neglected all her household chores and no longer shared her husband's bed.

That summer word got around that Chrysavyi was pregnant, and she was so big that it looked as if she were expecting twins, so that everyone felt sorry for her and whenever the women met her they would wish her a safe delivery. To Diamando this was all extremely galling, although she did not show it . . .

It was now October once again, two years since Chrysavyi's wedding, the harvest in Daphnyla was another modest one, and the time was fast approaching when Yoryis would be discharged and return to his village. Everyone in Stathis' household was on edge, afraid of what the future might bring.

One morning Diamando woke up very early with the uneasy feeling that Stathis and Chrysavyi had not returned home that night; crossing herself, she rapidly got dressed, left the children and hurried down the path towards the hut. On reaching it she heard groans coming from within. Diamando's heart now started beating violently; she tried to enter but found the door bolted from within. Without further hesitation she tore away part of the wattle wall and forced her way inside. There she found her husband sitting in one corner of the hut and her daughter-in-law lying on a pile of dry bracken in the other, her face pale and looking gravely ill. Stathis stared up at her fearfully, his face ravaged, while Chrysavyi's groans increased, her whole body writhing in pain.

'What's going on?' Diamando demanded, shaken to the core and glaring fiercely now at Stathis now at the sick woman.

Neither of them replied and her frightened daughter-in-law suppressed a groan, whereupon Diamando cried furiously, 'Die, you bitch!' and turning to her husband cowering in the corner added, 'Incestuous monster!' For several moments she did not say another word, then after brooding for a while she shouted at them balefully, 'What did I tell you? God never lets such crimes remain a secret!'

The sick girl wailed aloud, then biting her homespun dress cried out in anguish, 'Let me die! I want to die, but not like this, not like a dog!'

'Don't shout,' said Stathis in a hoarse undertone, 'if someone hears, we're doomed.'

'You're doomed because you've sinned,' replied Diamando.

'That heathen,' cried Chrysavyi, feeling her pains easing for a moment, 'is going to leave me to die like a dog and he'll let my baby perish too.' And she burst into tears.

Stathis crawled across to her and, still on his knees, put his hand over her mouth and said, 'Keep your voice down, soon you'll give birth and no one will be any the wiser; Diamando is going to help.' And he thought to himself, 'Just as well I brought her down here, in the village what would have become of us? But on the other hand, who knows?'

'Your sins will be found out' said Diamando shaking her head. 'I'm not a midwife.'

'But you yourself don't want any gossip,' protested Stathis feeling ashamed. 'After the child is born I'll take it into town and leave it at the orphanage. Here we'll say that she miscarried.'

'God won't just do what you want,' said Diamando shrugging her shoulders dubiously.

'Have pity,' begged Chrysavyi, looking up at her with tear-filled eyes.

'How long ago did her pains start?' asked Diamando.

'Midday yesterday,' said Stathis.

'Why then, impious man, did you not call someone? It's her first child and the birth will not be easy. She needs a midwife.'

'Better let her die.'

'Ruthless monster! Do you want two souls on your conscience? Have you the heart to let her die a sinner unconfessed, the baby unbaptized?'

'He has a heart of stone,' said Chrysavyi groaning with pain, 'but I'll go and give birth in the village square to shame him as he deserves.' And frantically she tried to get to her feet, but a sharp pain forced her to lie down again.

'I'll fetch the midwife,' said Diamando firmly and opened the door.

'I must hide first,' cried Stathis wildly.

'You must reap the seed you've sown,' she replied as she left the hut.

'Bless you and your children,' Chrysavyi called after her, her eyes filling with tears, 'I'm sorry I have caused you so much grief.'

'You can hear her groaning,' said Diamando re-entering the hut with the midwife. 'Naturally,' replied the newcomer, a thin elderly ugly woman, carelessly dressed but with a lively eye and lean capable hands, adding dispassionately, 'She's in a lot of pain.' Then after bidding Stathis good evening, she set about examining the expectant girl.

'The birth canal is open,' she said after a while, and leaving the patient she came over to Diamando, who was standing with arms folded in the middle of the hut, and explained in a hushed tone, 'Giving birth is difficult in the sixth month, because the baby has not yet turned inside the womb;* may God help the poor girl, but I fear the child won't live to be baptized.'

'Let the tree be saved,' said Stathis approaching the two women and looking at Diamando with a touch of admiration, 'it can produce another crop.' Then wearily he made for the door and sat down outside the hut.

'Callous wretch,' thought Diamando, giving him a sidelong glance.

He did not re-enter until four hours later, when he heard the whining of the newborn child. He was full of solicitude and concern about the future. Chrysavyi had been safely delivered but now looked pale and emaciated lying with her head propped up on a high pillow, her eyes closed, her hands clasped over her bosom like a corpse. She was fully dressed, as there was no bedding in the hut.

Diamando tore up an old shirt to use as swaddling for the child, which the midwife sitting on the ground had covered with her skirt.

'What a whopper,' said the midwife shaking her head, and turning to Stathis added, 'It's a boy!'

'Yes,' replied Diamando gravely, 'but it's premature so won't survive!' and she sighed, a warm tear rolling down her cheek. 'Poor hapless creature!' she reflected.

The old midwife looked at her in disbelief and the young mother started wailing in a heart-wrenching high-pitched tone, then barely moving her pale lips asked, 'Is my baby really going to die? Where is it?'

The midwife finished swaddling it on her outstretched legs, then carefully getting to her feet placed it in the mother's lap.

'Oh, the poor little mite,' moaned Chrysavyi raising it tenderly to her breast and continuing to weep.

'It's premature,' Diamando repeated, looking glumly at the ground. 'Count the number of months since Easter. How can you expect it to survive?'

Stathis looked at his wife dumbfounded, her words searing his heart like drops of molten lead. The infant's helplessness and shrill plaintive cries had touched him deeply, he felt affection for the tender creature and wanted to take it in his arms and kiss it; indeed it occurred to him that he had not felt such affection from the start for any of his other children. Alarmed, he asked himself, 'Why is Diamando saying this? Could she be thinking of doing away with it?' The idea shook him to the core, he felt his hair stirring and he had an impulse to confess his shocking crime at once and save the frail innocent child's life. He opened his mouth to speak but felt so ashamed that no sound crossed his lips and he sat down in confusion. Then he realized that the midwife was looking at him, as if asking him suspiciously whether Diamando was telling her the truth; he felt a shiver run down his spine, his fingers tingled and despite himself he nodded, confirming what his wife had said; then he sighed despondently and a tear crept into his eye.

'Go and fetch the priest,' Diamando now told the midwife. 'It must not die unbaptized. And summon the girl's parents. They must be informed.' And as she said this she handed her a note.

The old woman smiled. 'I'll be as quick as I can,' she replied and left the hut.

By now Chrysavyi had lapsed into unconsciousness.

'Make her some coffee,' Diamando said to her husband and lowering her eyes added with a sigh, 'I'm not going to let her suckle it.' Then she left the hut to gather herbs she knew of that would disperse the milk.

Stathis obeyed with tears in his eyes; he lit a fire and put water on to boil, then gazed despondently at the pale tormented figure of Chrysavyi, who though still unconscious was now shivering convulsively, her eyelids fluttering and her mouth distorted. 'Ominous signs,' he said to himself fearfully as he knelt down beside her. The swaddled infant, tiny and red faced, was fast asleep and Stathis gazed at it fondly, noting all its features. 'Poor little mite, poor little mite,' he murmured and without taking his eyes off it kissed its forehead gently. Then Chrysavyi groaned, a little colour appeared in her cheeks, and opening her eyes and turning to Stathis she murmured tremulously, 'Keep your child. Take care of him. Don't kill the poor thing!'

He did not reply, stung to the quick by what she had said. A moment later, raising her hand to her brow, she continued, 'Take it away and give it to strangers, how is it to blame for its illicit parents?'

He shook his head sadly. 'Who would I give it to?' he pleaded. 'Everyone will know that you have given birth. It's all in the hands of fate!'

'You too want to kill it,' she said, 'so that you'll all be rid of it.' She groaned again and sank back, shivering convulsively.

Soon Dimando returned, the herbs wrapped in her hanky, and put more water on to boil; then she poured some coffee and brought it over to the sick woman. But when she looked at her she realized that she had a raging fever.

'I think she's going to die,' she said wiping the girl's brow and trying to spoon some hot coffee into her mouth.

Stunned, Stathis did not say a word.

'Her teeth are clenched,' Diamando went on, 'and she's shaking all over. The fever seems to have gone to her brain.'

A moment later the midwife returned to the hut with the priest, a tall handsome fellow with a full black beard, the same man who had officiated at Chrysavyi's wedding, both of them looking very grave.

'Good gracious me,' exclaimed the priest on seeing the sick mother, who was shaking convulsively and moving her lips in an effort to say something, and then added, 'Your daughter-in-law is in a bad way, I must hear her confession as soon as we've finished with the baptism.' And he started putting on his vestments.

'I couldn't find her parents,' said the midwife, 'but I left word for them to come the moment they get back.' After a pause she added, looking at the sick woman, 'Chrysavyi's going to die, the fever's gone to her brain, poor thing! . . . Maria, Demos' daughter, died the same way just the other month.'

'All the emotional stress has been too much for her,' thought Diamando with a deep sigh and wiped away a tear.

Then the sick girl regained consciousness and opened her eyes, though still shivering as violently as ever. 'Ah, my head,' she moaned, 'it's torturing me.' Then recognizing the priest's face she smiled and with an effort raised herself on her elbow. 'I'm going to die,' she said faintly, 'will God have mercy on me?'

'Have hope,' replied the priest with tears in his eyes and motioned the others to withdraw.

'Don't dismiss them,' cried Chrysavyi, 'I'll confess my sins before them, they know them all already. They are lying to you, Father! I conceived it with my father-in-law! . . . And now they want to kill it.' She slumped back and lost consciousness again.

'Dirty lecher,' said the priest to Stathis, shocked and angry, 'they did no worse in Sodom. God have mercy on her soul and on his people.'

'Pay no attention to her,' said Diamandio, 'she is delirious!'

'I understand,' the priest apologized, turning pale, and proceeded to baptize the child . . .

Then he said, 'I'll go and fetch the sacraments,' and disappeared.

But Chrysavyi never regained consciousness even to receive the last rites. All afternoon she lingered on, her whole body convulsed, the whites of her eyeballs showing, her breathing irregular, her arms, legs and tongue twitching spasmodically. Towards evening her parents arrived at the hut and wept and lamented over her. Then she fell into a deep sleep and at midnight gave up the ghost without a struggle.

'She's gone,' announced the midwife with a sigh.

'She is at peace,' replied Diamando weeping.

But the child clung to life for another nine days, as the father fed it sugar-water and goats' milk, and on the ninth day, reduced to skin and bones and smaller than at birth, it died of malnutrition.

It was already buried beside its mother when Yoryis wrote from town to say that he was returning to the village, whereupon Stathis like some itinerant madman left the region and no one in Daphnyla ever learned what had become of him.

Krasades, Summer 1906

TWO LOVES

'Paints are getting more expensive, the cost of living's rising, and people pay less and less for my work.'

Such were the icon painter's thoughts (his name was Aryiris Spatharos) as he sat beside a table with his fine brush, touching up the eyes of a smoke-blackened Saint Nicholas they had brought to him at dawn for restoration. And as he went on painting he reflected, 'Praise the Lord, I've never been hard up, but people used to be willing to pay more, and yet my skills have been improving.'

He turned and gazed at the wall behind him. Numerous pictures were hanging on display there, several of his own among them, and as he looked critically at these he nodded, confirming his appraisal. 'There's no question,' he said to himself, 'my current technique's far better.'

Then putting his brush aside, he picked up the icon he was working on and held it at arm's length. 'It's just about ready,' he decided, scrutinizing it carefully. 'If there are still small blemishes, they can be touched up on site. After all, it's not a new piece, and my labour is more than worth the chicken they brought round.'

He rose and started pacing up and down the room. As he was not wearing shoes, his footsteps on the floor were barely audible. He was tall, thin and slightly stooped, with long white hair cascading over his shoulders. He dressed in peasant clothes, though at home he wore only a white shirt open at the chest, old patched baggy trousers* and slippers with no heels.

'It's still quite early,' the artist reflected. 'I might do a bit of work on the large icon.'

Wiping his brow with the back of his wrinkled hand, he looked around the room. Hanging on the whitewashed walls all the way to the rafters were innumerable icons, some antique, others more recent, still others freshly painted. In the case of the more ancient ones the colours were faded, the lines stiff and the workmanship crude and careless, as the artist who had done them was born in the remote past when studying art was difficult and good teachers non-existent or very hard to come by. This artist, the great-grandfather of Aryiris' own great-grandfather, had been dead for some time, at least two centuries; his bones would by now have turned to dust in the village cemetery where he had found his final refuge, driven out of Epirus by the Turks,* arriving in a wretched state, with nothing but the clothes on his back and hands unfit for manual labour . . .

Other icons hanging there were of finer quality, and still others even more recent and accomplished, all of them depicting saints, ascetics, martyrs, or apostles and all painted by the sons and grandsons of that first artist; there was even a small Saint Basil among them, painted by Aryiris when he was a lad and still learning his craft from his own father. The painter gazed at it thoughtfully a while and smiled as he recalled his youth, his marriage and his long departed father, whose words had always been so full of kindness, piety and faith in God's benevolence; in particular he recalled how his father used to tell him about the family's hereditary craft, which (as he in turn had heard from his own father and grandfather) their distant ancestor had brought with him from Epirus to the little Corfiot village, when the rampaging Turks had resolved to purge the world of Christianity. He had been a martyr both to religion and to art, this remote progenitor. Yet he was no more than an innocent victim and the Turks in their fury no more than an instrument of divine justice. The ruined and deserted village desecrated by the Turks had sinned, and God had resolved to make an example of it by wiping it from the face of the earth.

The painter smiled again as he examined his first tentative attempts, and recalled how he had worked beside his father, who would advise and guide him while continuing to work himself. And the smile on his lips suddenly became a chuckle as it occurred to him that, were his late lamented father alive today, he would be able to give him more than a few tips himself. Yes, his own technique seemed to him decidedly superior. He now cast his eyes across the room to the corner by the window, where the large icon he was still working on stood almost finished. It was a depiction of the Annunciation. The colours were fresh and gleaming; the face of the white-robed archangel, hovering on extended pinions and inclining forward with the beautiful white lily, was absolutely exquisite and his red lips almost seemed to speak; while the Virgin, kneeling humbly beneath a canopy of gold, her small figure swathed from head to toe in azure robes, really seemed to be listening to the archangelic greeting. Yet the archangel's face bore a striking resemblance to that of a youth who frequently visited the artist's home, and the Virgin's to that of a young woman of the neighbourhood; the artist, alone in his village, had thus discovered one of the secrets of his craft that his forebears, following traditional methods, had never understood.

Then suddenly his face darkened. He shook his head sadly and, still looking at the picture, murmured, 'Am I to be the last artist in the village?'

He remembered how his father had instructed him to pass on the skill to his children, and his children to theirs, as their ancestors had done since time immemorial, and he sighed. After a while he continued his reflections.

'The rest of the villagers cannot become artists, it's not in their nature. From father to son they have tilled the earth, and tillers they must remain, that's the way God has ordained things. Whereas we have been artists since the world began. My son ought to become an artist too. A pity he's our only child. But he won't even consider it, he doesn't fancy the sedentary life, nor has he an eye for colour — in that respect, he's just like his mother!'

He shook his head again. Then he took up a bundle of brushes and his palette and, standing in front of the painting, mixed his colours and settled down to work again. Meticulously he touched up the archangel's features, adding highlights here and there, refining the work he had done the previous day and trying to focus on the task at hand. But today he felt despondent and somehow could not concentrate. His son simply refused to listen to his arguments and wanted nothing to do with the family's hereditary vocation.

'Ah yes!' he reflected, resuming his earlier train of thought, 'he's not like us, and in other respects too he takes after his uncles,' and he sighed gloomily.

It was noon. From the stairs leading up to the artist's studio came the sound of heavy footsteps, and at once the head and torso of Aryiris' wife appeared. Her hair under her black headscarf was white but her face, though very wrinkled, was by no means ugly and her eyes beneath her tired brow were lively.

'What is it, Eftymia?' asked the artist without looking at her and continuing to paint.

'He's back,' the woman replied. 'You've completely forgotten about lunch today.'

Aryiris smiled. Putting his brush and palette on the floor, he stepped back and took another look at his painting, nodding complacently. And his wife watching in silence from the stairs, adjusted her headscarf, crossed herself and then as she did every day exclaimed, 'Most holy Virgin, you are truly alive.'

Aryiris was by now washing his hands in a dirty earthenware basin in the corner. As he did so he asked her, 'What's your son been up to?'

'Why always so censorious, in God's name?' she replied plaintively. 'Isn't he your son too?'

'Because he takes after others,' he sighed. 'I shall be the last artist in the village. Today he hasn't so much as ground my colours.'

'Even if he's not cut out for art,' replied the old woman irritably, descending a step, 'he's a good hard-working lad. He has his own plot and looks after it, and that will provide him with a living. Not everybody can be an artist! The Almighty knows what he's about.'

'It's with such remarks, such flattery, you've spoiled him,' he sighed. 'Art requires hours of hard sedentary work. But such has been my lot in life.'

His wife did not try to defend herself lest she upset him before lunch; after a pause the artist, wiping his hands on a rag, enquired, 'What have you been cooking?'

'Lamb for us, as it's Easter,' she replied humbly, 'but since you're fasting in honour of the Virgin,' she added, indicating the painting, 'I've put out bread and olives too especially for you.'

'Good,' he said well satisfied and then asked, 'Is our son downstairs?'

'Yes,' she replied, 'and he can hear us.'

'My remarks won't do him any harm,' he replied smiling.

Both now went downstairs. In a row along the wall by the door were three different sized wine casks on their stands, and next to them two greasy stone jars, one containing oil the other olives. On the opposite wall, facing the open door, was a table with benches either side, and on it a single plate of olives and a round flat cob of bread. In the chimney corner a huge fire was blazing and a blackened copper pot suspended from an iron trivet was bubbling and steaming. Sitting on a log beside the fire was the artist's son, carefully stirring the pot as he waited for his parents; he had just tasted the food with the ladle to see if it needed more salt and was still savouring the morsel. He was a young man of twenty with a small dark moustache and, like all the younger people of the village, was clad in western clothes.

'Hello, Father,' he said turning towards the stairs and smiling .

'Welcome, Yoryis,' replied his father warmly, as he sat down at the table and slowly crossed himself.

Without further ado, Yoryis poured the food into a deep bowl and, as the old man was slicing the golden cornmeal loaf, carried it over to the table and sat down opposite him, while his mother fetched a jug of wine mixed with water and a single mug and sat down beside her son. The peppery red stew was piping hot and smelt delicious. Mother and son crossed themselves, each took a slice of the bread the father had shared out, and all three began to eat.

The old man chewed his bread and olives slowly with his rotten teeth; the other two helped themselves to the lamb stew in the deep bowl, taking turns with the spoon and dunking their bread in the peppery red juice.

'Father,' said the young man, having satisfied his immediate hunger, 'are you sure you won't try a little stew?'

'No, my lad,' he replied, 'finish my share between you. What would be the point in breaking my fast now? When I was young I enjoyed the good life, but I vowed to the Virgin, hallowed be her name, that I'd fast until I'd finished painting her, and with her aid I will soon complete the icon, which will perform miracles for Christian folk.'*

'It will indeed,' said Yoryis, piously lowering his eyes, 'everybody in the village says so and no wonder.'

'Considering the devotion with which he's painting her,' concurred the old woman, wiping her lips with the edge of the woollen tablecloth, 'what else could one expect? I'm sure he's seen the Virgin in his dreams, because in the icon she really comes to life. Even so,' she added after a pause, 'I'm afraid it's no longer easy for him, now he's getting old.'

'Yes,' affirmed the artist gravely, pouring wine into the mug, 'it will perform miracles (unlike those icons peddled in town by the accursed Jews*) and people will revere it; my name will remain immortal in the village and strangers will come to kneel before the icon and do homage to the Virgin.'

'All you say is true enough,' she piously agreed, 'but shouldn't you look after your own health as well?'

'What difference does it make,' he replied, 'whether I live ten days or even a year more or less? My time will soon be up. But even my ancestors never painted pictures like this, though their works adorn every church on the island, from Sidari to Alefki,* and beyond.' And raising the mug to his lips a moment later, he added, 'To your health,' then drank.

The three of them continued their meal. After a while the old man remarked, 'Everything is going well, but I feel sick at heart, not because I'm awaiting death but because I am the last artist in the village.' He looked reproachfully at his son who had just refilled the mug and now raised it, saying, 'To your health, dear parents.'

'To your heath,' they both replied.

After draining the last drop, Yoryis answered the old man, his eyes downcast, 'I'm just not interested in painting, Father. It's not my fault.'

'Because you're more interested in other matters,' replied his father mildly, 'girls for instance . . .'

'And so he should be at his age,' said his mother leaping to his defence, 'soon he'll be getting married, just as you did.'

'I too was young then,' said the old man shaking his white head, 'and my late lamented father was alive, remember, Eftymia? I was apprenticed to him, worked at our craft and received his blessing. Sunday observance every week, holidays just once a year, and we would celebrate with the whole village.'

'How can you complain about your son? Doesn't he cultivate his plot?'

'A tiller of the soil,' sneered the old man.

'He'll make more than a good living out of it,' replied the mother.

'I have no other trade,' sighed Yoryis.

'I'm concerned about you,' said his father, 'I don't like you gadding about all day. What do you get up to? The village has become another Sodom these days.'

'Arrange a marriage for him,' said the mother, 'then he'll settle down and spend more time at home. You yourself got married, didn't you?'

'I did indeed, but in compliance with my parents' wishes. And I fully intend to find him a respectable young girl. But he must have a little patience. Our family has always formed alliances with notables and priests.'

'And Yoryis will be no exception,' said the mother, glancing proudly at her son.

But now Yoryis flushed with anger. Day after day the old man would weary him with his advice and his complaints. Was it his fault if he was not cut out to be an artist, if his hands were inept at holding brushes, mixing colours or touching up saints' features? If God had given him that gift he would have used it. But on the contrary he felt drawn to and captivated by the outdoor life, by hunting, by hard work with shovel, hoe and plough, by the toil and sweat of manual labour and the struggle with the stubborn earth that only yielded to rough blows, as if desiring to be ravished before delivering her bounty. He marvelled as the seedlings sprouted and the meadows turned a tender green, and later on his heart rejoiced when the well-nourished corn shot up producing thick firm cobs; then as he pricked them with his nail to release the milk that would become sweet bread, he had the gratifying feeling that the earth's bounty was the work of his own hand. Surely this honest labour, capable of feeding both his aged parents and himself, was at least as sacred as his father's painting? And wasn't it more useful to society? Every village thrives without an artist, but not one without manual labour. And wasn't the care-free existence of the labourer much easier and more agreeable than the mad enthusiasms of the icon painter? And then being shut up at home, the stench of paint, and the finicky detailed work that tires the eyes, benumbs the brain and wearies the spirit, ah, all that was not for a young man longing to yield to the intoxication of his youth.

To be out of doors in summer under the baking sun, when the warm air seemed to quiver above the meadows and the vineyards, or among the massive olive trees where the whispering leaves would kiss as their heavy branches brushed against each other in the breeze, or in autumn among vineyards laden with ripe grapes under a clear blue sky, or in the chilly winter season, or in springtime when all creation was suffused with the fragrance of flowers — ah, that was the life for him, that was what his heart exulted in!

And then there was the sound of maidens singing in the olive groves as he roamed the parish boundaries hunting birds, and the companionship of friends in the evening after a hard day's work, and the dancing, singing and festivities, and the tippling in village wine-stores, ah, how could he sacrifice all that to shut himself away in dusty solitude mixing foul-smelling colours, painting icons and contemplating ancient legends, when outside life and happiness were calling.

So now the young man felt resentful listening yet again to his father's admonitions, fully aware of what the old man was leading up to, that there was something else he was aggrieved about. But he reminded himself that people of his father's generation were very different from the youth of today, naturally enough since they had grown up under a different government with different laws, and had been taught to respect things that cut no ice today and were ridiculed by the young or middle aged. As regards marriage, young people no longer complied with their parents' wishes, but took the girl they fancied and were commended for it by their peers. Yoryis could think of so many friends about his age who had married the girl of their choice and rightly disregarded the opinion of their father and mother, since they were the ones who had to live with their wives and not their parents.

It was on the tip of Yoryis' tongue to say this, but in the end he didn't dare and after a pause merely remarked, 'Don't complain about me, Father. As I've told you, I'm not cut out for art, so let me live the way I want. You know I'm a hard worker and capable of earning my own living. I'll be able to help you both, as well as raising a family once married.'

'So we're up for marriage this year, are we!' replied the old man with an irritating laugh. 'We're drowning in wealth of course. The house bursting at the seams with customers. Our bough's about to split under the bounteous crop! Sixty lousy fivers* is all the wardens at the Church of the Annunciation are paying for their icon!'

'You're not taking into account,' said the young man humbly and a little cowed, 'that the grain bins are all full and that Mother has a stocking full of fivers in her trunk.'

'They're tenners, not fivers,' replied the old man peevishly.

'The Lord be praised, we're not as poor as you make out,' observed the mother. 'Yoryis is now twenty-two and I've grown old. The lad is right, we need a younger woman around the place, and you must find him one, whomever God inspires you to select.'

The old man laughed again and shaking his head made no reply. But Yoryis now lost patience.

'Mother,' he declared, 'I'll find a wife myself. I intend to marry somebody I fancy.'

'We know that,' replied the artist curtly, a frown darkening his wrinkled brow. 'You've set out on an evil path. You've found two already — which one do you intend to choose?'

Yoryis blushed and lowered his eyes shamefacedly.

'What's this your father's saying?' asked his mother anxiously.

'Listen, Yoryis,' the old man went on, 'don't yield to temptation. I don't like either of them, and one's not free, so why get mixed up with her?'

'It's the girl I want! The other woman is our go-between.'

'D'you think I was born yesterday?' his father observed gravely. 'You're lying to me, which does you no credit, and you're sailing into murky waters. For your own good, I don't want you visiting either one again.'

'But I really like the girl,' he replied staunchly.

'You're not bringing just any chance acquaintance here. I must like your wife as well.'

'He's right,' agreed the mother, raising her head a little and adjusting her headscarf. 'We must both approve of her! We need a woman who will look after us in our old age, not one who will bury us before our time. Otherwise he won't give you his consent!'

'Come now, Mother,' said Yoryis impetuously, remembering his friends, 'those rules applied under the British. Now every young man does as he pleases.'

'That's what wastrels tell you in the wine-store,' said the old man, his hackles rising. 'You're up to no good, but watch out or you'll receive my curse.'

'No, no,' exclaimed the mother in alarm, 'don't curse our only son. The Lord above hears every word you say.'

'Instead of grinding my colours for me,' the old man went on querulously, 'instead of learning our ancestral craft, you go chasing after fillies! Is this how we brought you up, is this your true character?'

Yoryis kept quiet.

'He's right,' agreed the mother.

'I'll find a wife for you,' said the old man.

'No,' he replied defiantly, 'I shall marry somebody I love.'

'Both of them have caught you in their snares,' exclaimed the old man angrily. 'Our village has become another Sodom. But watch your back. Women are not alone in the world, they have brothers and clansmen jealous of their honour. They have their eye on you already. You're misbehaving and bringing shame on us.'

Yoryis blushed. How had his father discovered all his secrets? The old man looked at him searchingly and the mother now listened anxiously with growing curiosity.

'I know all about it,' the artist continued after a pause. 'You think you can pull the wool over my eyes. You're not behaving honourably. You're cheating the girl so you can enjoy the married woman and let people think she is your go-between.'

'The married woman?' said Yoryis, going even redder.

'Yes,' replied the old man, 'you've forgotten both your father and God's way and are keeping company with trollops.'

'Who are you referring to?' asked his son defensively, his eyes downcast. 'Maria, Theodosis's daughter, may be poor but she's an honest girl.'

'If she were the only one, I wouldn't have said anything. But the other woman is your mistress at the same time. I won't mention her by name, but you're asking for trouble!'

Yoryis sighed impatiently.

'How can you behave like this?' exclaimed his mother, visibly upset.

'Pay no attention,' he replied, 'Father's suspicions are completely groundless.'

But his agitation was quite obvious. He got up from the table, strode about the house, sat down on the log seat by the fire, got up again almost at once and finally took his gun down from the wall and made for the door.

'Off hunting again?' his father remarked sarcastically.

But Yoryis pretended not to hear and hurried out. The old man, who meanwhile had finished his frugal meal, crossed himself, stood up and turned to go back upstairs to his icons. But pausing for a moment he said to his wife, who had gone very pale and was standing there as if turned to stone, 'You see, Eftymia? It's in the blood, he's behaving just like your brothers used to. Where will it all end?'

'Who's the other woman?' his wife asked in a subdued voice.

'I'm not going to name her,' he replied. 'May God make him see sense. You try to talk to him.'

The old man did not wait for her reply and slowly climbed the stairs to his room, anxious to press on with his Annunciation.

Yoryis, his gun on his shoulder, ran helter-skelter through the garden and down the steep hillside, then stopped for a moment undecided, heaving a sigh as if just released from an oppressive nightmare, and looked about. Now at last he could feel free. Below him in a narrow dell between the hill on which the village stood and the one opposite, a late crop of well-watered corn was swaying in the breeze, its broad leaves still gloriously fresh. At this distance the surrounding hills, covered with silvery-green olive trees shimmering in the midday sun, looked quiet and peaceful and appeared to beckon to him. Unconsciously he shifted his gun to the other shoulder and set off down a familiar path, which after winding down the hillside from the village and cutting across the field of corn and another of tobacco, brought him to the foot of the hill opposite where he entered the olive grove.

He slackened his pace and, holding his gun in both hands across his chest, looked about as he proceeded. Peering through the leaves in the hope of spotting a bird he started up the hill, advancing steadily from olive tree to olive tree, and as he climbed he ruminated.

His father was angry with him and justly so. He was right, but he was wrong as well. He wanted him to be an artist, but God had not endowed him with the talent he had bestowed upon his forebears. So how was he to blame? In that respect then, his father was in the wrong. After all, if he wasn't cut out to be an artist, if he was nauseated by the smell of paint, if he couldn't stand being cooped up indoors with brush and pallette, if he knew he could not distinguish between colours (all those reds, greens, yellows, blues, and heaven knows what else), wouldn't he be better off devoting himself to work that suited him, to the struggle to subdue the soil he loved?

But he was diverted from this train of thought by a bird chirping feebly in a tree somewhere over to the right. Cautiously he turned and followed the sound. Peering up through the foliage he tried to spy where the bird was hiding, then slowly and stealthily, with knees bent and head and chest thrust back, he circled the tree. The bird chirped again directly above his head and stealthily Yoryis took one step back. He could see leaves stirring and stood quite still, holding his breath. The bird was pecking away at the unripe olives and Yoryis could now make out its tiny head. He began to cock his gun, but the bird heard the noise and sensing danger flew away with a little squawk, soaring aloft then swooping down and settling in another tree a little higher up the hill.

'Ah, bad luck,' he said to himself frowning with vexation, 'this year the birds are very wily. Not at all surprising. Even the village school children, scarcely weened, have guns these days.'

With this reflection he continued on up the slope after the thrush, secretly hoping he might see it and take another shot at it. And as he climbed his mind, today refusing to focus solely on the hunt, flitted from one thought to another, as he mulled over the worrying circumstances of his life.

'Mother is getting on,' he told himself. 'With all the chores, they could really do with a woman around the house. And I need a woman even more urgently perhaps . . . If I go about things the right way and show a bit of tact, my father will let me marry whom I wish. There's no shortage of pretty girls I fancy in the village, and I could have my pick . . . But haven't I already chosen?'

'Which one?' a voice deep within him asked. 'Isn't what father says quite true? You're cheating the girl while enjoying the other woman as your mistress!'

'Have I decided on Maria,' he asked himself, 'or am I going to abandon her because she's poor and look elsewhere for someone with a fatter dowry and parents who are more respectable? No, it's Maria I've chosen. Maria is the one, and I know she loves me too, and others are aware that we're in love.'

'And what about the married woman,' came the voice from deep within, 'what are you going to do about her?'

'Well, even though we've had a rare old time together, I'll forget about her,' he said resolutely. 'Why bother with women who can never be entirely mine?'

And a moment later, after briefly reverting to the problems of hunting wily birds, he said to himself, 'Maria should be around here somewhere with her flock. Yesterday she promised she'd be waiting for me . . .'

'But the other woman could be about as well,' his gut instinct told him. 'She shadows Maria everywhere she goes these days . . .'

'So what if she is,' he answered. 'I'll get rid of her once and for all. I won't look at her again.'

'But why?' the voice deep within persisted. 'She's gorgeous, she's easy, she's willing. If you like you can sleep with her tonight. That's all she ever thinks about.'

'No!' he murmured to himself. 'Enough of such lewd thoughts. Why has my soul such evil impulses? Maria will become my wife . . .'

'And what's to prevent you,' the voice interjected, 'bedding one and marrying the other later?'

'Ah,' he thought ruefully, 'youth is hot-blooded and its own worst counsellor.'

But as he brooded over these matters, he again heard the bird chirping among the leafy branches of the olive tree he was passing under. He peered up through the leaves, noiselessly cocking his gun, and this time the bird did not take flight; overcome by hunger it was hastily and nervously pecking at the olives, shaking the branch and looking all around. Yoryis took aim and a moment later the sound of his gun rang out. The bird tumbled through the air and landed at Yoryis' feet, tweeting feebly and twitching with pain. Leaning on his gun the hunter, indifferent to its suffering, bent down and picked it up in one hand, then choked it between his finger and thumb and stuffed it in his pocket.

Then involuntarily he looked around.

A little further up the hill the bracken was rustling and stirring, as several sheep, tethered beneath an olive tree and startled by the shot, ran frantically in circles.

'Aha!' said Yoryis to himself, starting to reload. 'So they are here after all.' And as he rammed the wadding down the barrel of the gun, he looked about.

The girl was sitting at the foot of an olive tree, and as their eyes met they smiled. Yoryis shouldered his gun and walked towards her, calling out as he drew closer, 'Good day, Maria.'

She gave him a little wave with her fingers.

'What are you up to?' he asked, approaching.

'Darning,' she replied with an indifferent shrug, indicating the old clothes spread out across her thighs. Then with a winning smile she asked, 'What have you shot?'

'A thrush,' he replied, reaching into his pocket.

'How come they're so early this year?' she remarked. 'Though there still aren't many about.'

'Take it,' said Yoryis, producing the bird and dangling it by one leg in front of her.

'Why give it to me?' she asked him shyly.

'Because I love you,' he replied. 'You know that.'

The girl frowned, not holding out her hand to receive the dead bird, and said, ' Yoryis, what does your love bring me? Malicious gossip, and that I cannot bear.'

'Who's found out about us?' he asked anxiously.

'I don't know,' she replied sadly, adjusting her headscarf, 'but we're the talk of the town. I hardly dare walk through the square now. And with my parents and my brothers I feel so ashamed. Indeed I'm quite afraid of them.'

'That's very strange,' replied Yoryis with a grimace and thought to himself, 'The other woman must be stirring up trouble.'

'Kisses leave their mark,' she added gravely.

'How d'you mean?' he asked laughing.

For a moment she made no reply, then raising her dark eyes and looking at him, she sighed and said, 'If you're honourable, you should marry me. That will put an end to all the gossip and my family won't become embittered.'

'Yes,' he replied, nodding as if to confirm his promise, 'I will marry you.'

'When?'

'When my father consents.'

'But will he?'

'My mother respects you. The old man will soon come round. Here, take it.' And he dropped the thrush onto the garment she was mending.

For a while neither of them spoke, as if uncertain what they should do now. Then they looked at one another and smiled. Leaning on his gun, Yoryis, sat down cross-legged on the ground beside her.

The girl now looked around. 'Somebody might see us,' she said smiling, 'and then what will become of me? . . . But if they throw me out,' she added thoughtfully, 'I'll come and find you at your place!'

'I haven't seen anyone about,' he replied gazing into her eyes, 'how long have you been here?'

'Since dawn, but I haven't seen a soul either.'

'Who's going to come this way in the middle of the day?'

But as he said this it flashed through his mind that the other woman could be somewhere close at hand, as he suspected she might out of jealousy be lying in wait for them. Hadn't he better leave at once? But then again, it might be a good thing for her to see them together, because that way he'd be free of her once and for all. And anyway it wasn't even certain they'd be noticed by the other woman. So why leave? Aloud he said, 'Besides, what does it matter if anybody sees us?'

Maria shrugged again and gazed into his eyes.

But that look was enough to set Yoryis' blood coursing through his veins. Despite himself he seized her in his arms and kissed her, gently on the brow at first, then more ardently on the cheeks and finally with fervent passion on the lips and neck, pressing her head close to his broad chest. And as he kissed her he kept saying, 'I love you, you shall be mine, kiss me, kiss me too.'

Now carried away by love's tender passion also, she kissed him blushingly with passionate desire, surrendering her whole body to his ardent caresses. Such was the sweetness of the moment that they both forgot the world and time slipping by and thought only of their love for one another.

But it did not last long. A rustling in the grass nearby startled and alarmed them. Yoryis leaped to his feet at once and Maria, pale and frightened, lowered her headscarf over her face.

A good-looking woman of about twenty-eight emerged, tall and buxom with an ample bosom, barefoot and with her sleeves rolled up. Her face was pale and ominous. Standing in front of them without getting too close she burst into peels of loud derisive laughter. This frightened Maria even more, as she immediately suspected that her spiteful rival's hilarity might be a prearranged signal for others to appear, so she uncovered her head and without raising her eyes said to Yoryis in a trembling voice, 'Obviously we have now been seen, so take me home with you.'

'Be patient,' he said scowling, 'let's find out what she's up to first!'

The woman went on shrieking with laughter, but then started cursing and scolding them angrily as well: 'Look at the layabouts, the wastrels, skulking in the shadows to make love! You're the village laughing-stock, you know!'

'Why are you carrying on like this, Vasiliki?' said Maria trembling.

'You just couldn't control your lust, could you,' she answered glaring at her fiercely, 'you needed a man, and so you went out and found yourself one! That's the sort you are!' And raising her voice she continued, 'How about that! Maria, Theodosis's daughter, with the artist's son, ay! Underneath the olive trees in the middle of the day!'

'What's it got to do with you?' Maria asked her even more alarmed. 'For God's sake, Vasiliki, keep your voice down.' And looking tearfully at Yoryis she added, 'Come let's go, Yoryis, take me home with you.'

But Yoryis did not move. As if turned to stone he gazed indecisively at the other woman. He had not expected such brazenness from her. And Maria couldn't help thinking, 'The trollop must have her reasons for acting up like this.'

Vasiliki meanwhile went on screaming, 'So that's the sort you are, ay, Maria, Theodosis's daughter! And people think you're so saintly they'd take communion from your filthy hands!'

'Why are you abusing me?' Maria cried, feeling that she should defend herself, 'how have I offended you?' and she looked at Yoryis, appealing for his support.

Vasiliki became even more irate; her eyes blazed, she went red in the face and flinging her headscarf to the ground she shouted, 'You think he'll marry you, you vixen, don't fool yourself. Never. I won't let him!'

'What d'you mean, won't let him?' she replied, again looking reproachfully at Yoryis.

'You can be heard all round the hills,' he said nervously, 'calm down, both of you be on your way. We'll all be in trouble if you carry on like this.'

'Dishonest scoundrel,' Vasiliki screamed furiously, baring her foam-flecked teeth, her arms akimbo, 'you still have the face to talk! You cheated me and now you're trying to cheat this silly coot, promising her the earth. All lies, you know full well that none of it will ever happen! Even if everyone consents, I will not let it . . .'

'Don't shout,' Yoryis pleaded, trying to interrupt her.

But then Maria discovered a courage she did not know she possessed. She had never quarrelled in her life, but now fury got the better of her. What right, she thought, did this married woman have to talk to her like that and why did she think it in her power to destroy her happiness?

'What's it got to do with you, is it any skin off your nose if I love the painter's son?' she shouted, her cheeks flushing red. 'And you a married woman — why don't you sort out your own miserable life? You should be lamenting your own sad fate, instead of destroying the happiness of others out of jealousy and spite! Was it our fault that your husband left you?'

'Watch your tongue, you little whore!' replied the other, slapping herself on the thigh for emphasis. 'Who taught you to answer back like that? Well, blow me! The whole village knows I left my husband first, because he kept tormenting me with his string of little tarts, until his feuds and quarrelling obliged him to depart. As for you, I'll make sure you burst with frustration. Even if you swallow the cutlery you'll never marry Yoryis!'

'Have you no shame, Vasiliki?' cried Yoryis, who now felt that he was losing face. 'Do you want to cause bloodshed in the village. Don't you understand, we can be heard for miles around? Is this how a woman should behave in public?' And turning to Maria he said, 'Come, gather your sheep and let her vent her spleen, Maria. She's not in her right mind today.'

'She must have some reason for this outburst,' Maria told him, 'but what have I ever done to her?' And with tears in her eyes she untied her sheep and prepared to leave. But before setting off she said to the other woman, 'You're notorious all round the parish for playing the whore,

Vasiliki you baggage, seducing and defiling the young men!'

'There goes the pot calling the kettle black,' she replied spitefully. 'You say that because you're jealous. Yoryis belongs to me and you're not having him. He's going to leave you, so get stuffed! Get stuffed! Get stuffed!' And as she said this she thumped her palm repeatedly with her right fist. Then she added, 'The statutory time will quickly pass and I'll divorce that reprobate; then we'll get married and you'll end up with nothing but your shame, you'll watch us and you'll wilt. So get stuffed! Get stuffed!' And she went on pounding her palm with her fist.

'This must stop,' said Yoryis firmly. 'Listen, Vasiliki. You're up to no good and trying to provoke bloodshed. I don't want you. I never want to set eyes on you again. You must forget about what happened between us. Why torment the girl?'

But Maria, devastated, shook her head. 'So that's it,' she said. 'Everything she says is true then? You slept with her and cheated her? So that's the sort of man you are?' She felt utterly miserable and sick at heart. And as she set off towards the village she gave him a fiery look and cried, 'You fraud! Go and live with your common whores. You won't see me again.' And tugging her sheep behind her angrily, she hurried off down the hill.

'Dirty bitch,' shouted the other woman after her, determined to have the last word, 'd'you think you're any better? Didn't I just catch you making love to Yoryis right here under the olive tree? Now go and show your face in the village. Your reputation precedes you. Why else d'you think I was hollering like that!'

'Don't you have a grain of sense, woman?' Yoryis scolded her. 'That's enough for one day. Do you want two people on your conscience, her as well as me?' And with this he set off after Maria. 'The way things have turned out,' he said to himself, 'it would be best to take Maria home with me at once. Then this rumpus will die down and the whole village won't be in an uproar.'

But Vasiliki, cocking her head archly in mock admiration, barred his way, saying, 'So where is Mr Yoryis off to now?' Then she continued more aggressively, 'Didn't you promise me you'd leave her for my sake? Isn't that what you promised? And now you've changed your mind, I suppose? Well, you're fooling yourself if you really think I'm going to let you off the hook. I've made up my mind, I'm going to follow the two of you about and denounce you from the rooftops. D'you understand?'

Maria meanwhile was retreating hastily, driving her sheep before her. Her mind was in confusion, her head was aching and her eyes were brimming with tears. By now the trees on the hillside were obscuring her from view and soon she disappeared. 'Ah, poor lass,' sighed Yoryis, looking at the bird he had given her earlier lying on the ground. 'She's even left the thrush behind.'

'Of course! Love tokens at a time like this!' mocked Vasiliki.

'Clear off, you shameless hussy,' he replied angrily, 'I never want to see your face again!'

'You're the one who made me so and now you have the gall to curse me! Who told you to go cheating on me! What have I done to deserve your scorn?'

'And what harm had that poor girl done you?'

'She'd have married you! I wish all three of us were dead. But I started caterwauling so that everyone would know. And I've succeeded. Look!' And she pointed through the trees towards the hilltop.

'Murderess!' he snarled at her with suppressed rage, biting his lip as he stared at the handful of women and children who had gathered to observe the quarrel and were watching them and listening intently, talking secretly amongst themselves. 'What have you gained by this?' he added bitterly.

And with that he hastily set off down the hill, reflecting with alarm that the whole village would shortly hear about the embarrassing affair.

'She's not going to enjoy you either,' the woman shouted after him, 'and don't think I'm going to leave you two in peace!'

But Yoryis was by now running and did not pause to listen. He was overwhelmed with shame. Why hadn't he listened to his father? How could he ever show his face at home or in the village?

The following day the artist rose early and, after reading from the scriptures like the priests, immediately settled down to work on his icon and by noon had finished it. Now, still holding his brushes, he was standing back to look at it.

His face was pale and gaunt, his long hair unkempt (his wife had not combed it for him that morning as she usually did), the bones of his cheeks and chin protruded and his eyes were bleary. But on the icon the fresh paint gleamed lustrously. The exquisite figure of the Virgin, swathed from head to foot in dark blue robes, was kneeling beneath a golden canopy, her head inclined, her eyes downcast; while opposite her the radiant archangel, clad in white and hovering on extended wings, seemed to be murmuring 'Hail, Mary' with his modest lips, as he offered her the pure white lily, his earnest innocent face full of reverence for the Mother of God.

The artist scrutinized the large icon with meticulous care — every brush-stroke, every line, every fold in every garment, right down to the light reflected in the angel's flaxen hair and the bright haloes round the heads of the two figures — and whenever his eye strayed to the other icons hanging on the walls painted by his forbears, he would reflect that his own was superior to them all.

He smiled, but the smile soon faded. His face, haggard from hard work, self-discipline and fasting, looked unusually grave today and his mind was beset by worries.

That reprobate only son of his, who had broken with the family's traditions and become the talk of the town through his dissolute behaviour, regarded with contempt by everyone and hostility by many, why couldn't he have taken after his esteemed and virtuous ancestors, why was he always getting into trouble? And where could he be now? Might his life not be in danger? But then how could a frail old man like himself assist him?

The artist gazed at the Virgin deeply troubled, a warm tear trickling down his withered cheek. 'Help him,' he sighed in supplication.

Despite himself he now began to listen to what was going on around him. As always, the sound of people going about their business entered through the window, something the artist normally never paid attention to. But today he had the impression that his son's name was on everybody's lips and that he was being slandered. He sighed again and shook his head sadly. From the familiar sounds downstairs he could tell that his wife was tidying the place and could even hear her mumbling, for the old woman had been accustomed to talking to herself from quite an early age. She too was preoccupied with Yoryis, worrying fretfully and fearing the worst. The artist sensed that the same sorrow burdened both their hearts. Putting his brushes on the table, he leaned out of the window. In the street immediately below the house, a few people were chatting casually but they did not look up. The usual hubbub was coming from the wine-stores. The old man looked to left and right, withdrew from the window, paced up and down the room, then crossed to the window overlooking the garden and looked out. And having failed to see what he was hoping for, he resumed his seat before the icon.

'Still no sign of him,' he thought. 'Not a soul has seen him since yesterday. I'm ashamed to face people.' A moment later, as if his conscience were troubling him, he said to himself, 'If I'd known things were going to take this course, I might have intervened in time. But who could have imagined he would turn out like this? Suddenly the devil's on his back! The wrath of God has found him out. If only he'd married Maria and quietened down. I'd have given my consent, what else could I have done! It's true I had higher hopes for him, I wanted him to be quite different, but when all is said and done his marrying Maria wouldn't have been so bad. I should have let him follow his bent, clod-busting with a hoe, at least he'd then have settled down at home with his family and looked after me and my long-suffering wife in our old age! . . . Now, God forbid, we may end up alone with no heir at all. People are so vindictive these days and I have grave misgivings! One thing I don't understand is why Maria refuses to become his wife.'

He started listening again. The old woman was talking to somebody downstairs.

'Go on up and see him, Reverend,' she was saying.

A moment later the old man saw the village priest coming up the stairs. His face relaxed a little and he smiled.

'Good-day, Reverend,' he said, advancing to kiss the priest's hand, 'welcome.'

'Good-day, Aryiris,' replied the dark-robed priest extending his hand, a tall handsome man with a long fair greying beard, 'any news?'

'No end of worries,' replied the artist sadly, 'but please be seated, Reverend.'

The two men moved across to the icon, where instinctively the priest doffed his hat, crossed himself and murmured a prayer, before remarking, like everyone else who had seen the painting, 'You must have seen the Virgin and the angel in your dreams, Aryiris?'

'Her grace inspired me,' replied the artist modestly. 'I put all my skill, all my faith, all my devotion into it. The Virgin heard my plea.'

'Today they delivered the repository for your picture to the church' said the priest, as he donned his hat and sat down on a stool. 'It looks splendid now it's fixed in place. The whole village is expecting your icon to work miracles. Those who have seen it are awe-struck and amazed. The sick are devotees already. When we collect it, we'll bear it with candles and banners in procession to the church and sanctify the village. Shall we say next Sunday, to give the paint a chance to dry?'

'If that is what the village wishes,' said the artist bashfully, with secret pride.

'That is what the village both wishes and expects,' replied the priest stroking his greying beard. 'The villagers are proud of their shrine, which I imagine will remain a house of prayer and refuge for Christians to the end of time.' And after a pause he reluctantly added, 'Only a few hotheads are against it.'

'Against it?' asked the old man going pale and lowering his tired eyes. 'Why?'

'Because of your son,' replied the other quietly.

'But how is the icon to blame?' the artist exclaimed dejectedly. 'That son of mine has embittered my old age; he's entirely in the wrong, Reverend, but what am I to do?' And he wiped away a tear with his finger as it trickled down his cheek. Then he asked, 'Are there many of them? What have they in mind?'

Just then the old woman came upstairs carrying a round brass tray with a cup of black coffee, a measure of raki and a glass of water, and looking pale and anxious too, placed them before the priest, who then replied, 'I don't know if they have anything in mind, but they are against your family's receiving any kudos. Since yesterday, I've noticed Maria's brothers meeting up with Vasiliki's relations. They've never fraternized before, but no doubt the shame has decided them to make common cause.'

The old man shook his head dejectedly. His aged wife, taking off her headscarf and twisting it in her hands, said angrily, 'That wretch Vasiliki, may the Virgin' — with a nod towards the icon — 'confound her, she's the one responsible for this, she's been stirring up the village and is determined to bereave us.'

'But your son was misbehaving,' exclaimed the priest with an emphatic gesture.

'He was not the first,' replied the painter without raising his eyes.

'That woman,' said his wife with a sneer, 'she gives herself to anybody like the bitch she is. She's corrupted the whole village. Time and again they've seen her at it. All the women in the neighbourhood say so. Is my son to pay for all her sins?'

For a moment all three fell silent. The priest sipped his coffee, the old woman put her headscarf on again and the artist stared glumly at the icon.

'By the way, Aryiris,' the priest remarked after a while, taking up his glass of raki, 'I went round to see them as you requested.'

'And what did they say?' he asked anxiously.

'Theodosis is consumed with grief and shame and all his sons are outraged. They want to turn Maria out of the house and her mother has given her a hiding more than once; she's been beaten black and blue. But all to no avail. She won't have your son. He's far too dissolute, she says.'

'Is that the reputation our son has?' asked the father in distress, lowering his eyes in shame.

'Theodosis told me everything could be sorted out,' the priest continued thoughtfully, 'except that his daughter feels uncomfortable about entering such a distinguished family. It's not their destiny, he says, to become related to the saintly painter of miracle-working icons, and they'll be left to bear the shame for ever. But to be fair, Maria is partly right.' Then raising the glass of raki he said, 'Good health to both of you!'

'Give us your blessing, Reverend,' they replied sadly without looking at him.

'What now?' said the old woman looking at the painter.

'What indeed!' he replied shaking his head.

'Patience,' the priest exhorted them, 'all such trials are sent by God. Don't sigh and moan against him. It's not your destiny, Aryiris, to savour glory unalloyed by grief. Patience.'

'Confound the vixen,' said the old woman. 'She's determined to cause mischief.'

For a while the three of them again lapsed into silence. The artist sat deep in thought, his head resting in his hands, while the priest and the old woman looked at him and awaited his decision.

'I must send my son away,' the old man concluded finally, biting his pale lips. 'Here they may well kill him.'

'A sound idea,' the priest smilingly agreed. 'The Virgin has given you wise counsel. Trouble will be avoided in the village and the whole matter will blow over.'

'If they don't make a move first,' sighed the old man apprehensively.

'Sunday at eight we'll bear your icon of the Virgin to the church,' the priest concluded.

'As the village wishes,' replied the artist.

The priest got up to go. 'I'll bid you good-day, then,' he said holding his hand out to be kissed.

'Good-bye, Reverend,' they replied, 'and thank you for the favour.'

As he went down the stairs the priest added, 'He should emigrate!'

Now the old couple were alone. 'He's bereaved us,' said the old man gloomily.

'And in the village we're disgraced,' added the mother tearfully. 'But where could Yoryis be? We haven't set eyes on him since yesterday.'

'God only knows where he'll have got to. Perhaps he'll be in touch again! Ah, he's poisoned my life and my success, why did he have to choose this moment? But be off now and try the hut, scour the parish bounds and see if you can find him. There's not a moment to be lost. We must evade their wrath if things are not to get out of hand. My old legs are no longer up to it.'

'Yes,' she replied, 'I'll go at once.'

She hurried down the stairs, left the house and set off through the garden down the hill. Now alone, the artist went on brooding anxiously as he sat motionless on his stool, and every now and then he heaved a sigh. Meanwhile the sun had set and twilight had set in. But still Eftymia did not return. So far she had not found him.

It was night. Yoryis was alone in his hideaway, a hut made of sacking and bamboo and plastered inside and out with mud. Since the previous day he had not ventured into the village and had been lying low in out-of-the-way spots beyond the parish bounds, only returning to the hut after dark to sleep. He too was thinking he might leave. Because of this however his mother, who had been out looking for him, had by nightfall still not found him anywhere. Now the door to the hut was closed and barred; a fire was smouldering among the ashes in the hearth, the smoke from the logs rising towards the blackened bamboo rafters. He was restless and preoccupied and kept turning over in his mind how best to inform his parents of his resolve to leave, as he felt too ashamed to face them. Meanwhile he was preparing for bed, as it was getting late.

Then suddenly someone tapped lightly on the door outside, sending a shiver down his spine. Instinctively he glanced at his gun hanging on the wall above the bed, but he did not answer.

'Yoryis, Yoryis,' a voice said softly, accompanied by more knocking, 'are you asleep? Wake up!'

Yoryis recognized the voice with alarm. It was Vasiliki. 'Oh God,' he thought with dread, his heart pounding, 'what does she want now!' But he still did not reply.

'Wake up,' she repeated louder, 'wake up and open the door; it's for your sake that I've come.'

He did not answer and kept quite still, hoping the woman would perhaps think the door had been locked from the outside and go away.

But she again called out to him, rattling the door, 'Why won't you listen? Why won't you open up? I know you're inside. I can see the light, I can see the smoke escaping through the cracks. Open up, I tell you. I must see you!'

'What do you want now?' he replied. 'Haven't you caused enough trouble already?'

'Open up!' she commanded.

'No!' he replied stoutly.

'I'll set fire to the hut,' she told him stubbornly.

'Heartless woman!' he replied going over to the door.

'You're the one who's made me so,' she said. 'I insist you let me in! Don't waste time!'

He obeyed. The woman entered at once and bolted the door behind her. Yoryis sat down beside the hearth, poked the logs, added kindling to the smouldering embers and blew until they flickered into life.

'Why did you take so long to open?' she asked in a harsh angry voice.

He did not reply, nor did he look at her directly but went on tending the fire.

'D'you think,' she said coming over to him, 'I'm going to leave you in peace? Perhaps you still think you can marry your Maria?'

'Haven't you heard,' he replied dejectedly, 'she refuses even to see me.'

'The priest was acting as your go-between again today,' she told him. 'With time she may come round.'

'I've not been back to the village since you shamed me.'

'Things are coming to a head tonight! We must flee together to another life.'

'What, with you?' he said in alarm.

'If you value your life!' she replied promptly.

'No,' he told her firmly.

'Then we will both be killed tonight,' she replied. 'And no great loss, as far as I'm concerned. I can't bear my present life. I'm disgraced and treated with contempt, and you're to blame for everything.'

'Me?' he said, getting up from the hearth where the fire was now blazing. 'Everyone knows I was not the first. You always had a dubious reputation.'

'Because there were always others like you ready to take advantage of me. But there's no time to lose. My kinsmen will be here any minute.'

'Now what have you been up to?' he cried approaching, his hand raised as if to strike her. 'Why have you come here at this ungodly hour?'

'It's all your fault,' she replied calmly. 'If you'd left Maria there would have been no trouble. No one would have found out and we'd have led a charmed life. But you too tried to cheat me and that I couldn't bear. Let's go, I tell you!'

'No,' he repeated resolutely, 'I refuse to run away with you. I don't want anything to do with you. Why have you come?'

'Ah, then we're doomed!' she cried turning pale, her eyes wide with fear. 'If you'd seen the way they've been carrying on all day! They've been hunting for you high and low. They're after your blood. None of them will speak to me. They're saying they'll wash away the shame I've brought on them in one fell swoop. They'll kill us both. My kinsmen have joined forces with Maria's brothers. And they all are in a frenzy. Quick, let's go, let's go!

'Not with you, I said. I won't betray Maria.'

'Ah, she's the one you love! But your obstinacy will cost you your life.'

'Not even if you were a different person! Just think of everything you've done! Your reputation is notorious, you're another man's wife and your husband could get us thrown in jail as and when he pleased.'

'Come on,' she pleaded, 'they'll be here any minute.'

By the light of the fire blazing in the hearth she looked pale as she anxiously cast her eyes around the hut. The more time passed, the greater became the danger and the harder their escape.

'Let's go,' she reiterated tearfully. 'If you love your parents, let us go, I beg you! They are sure to find us. I swear to God, I'm telling you the truth.' A moment later she added, flaring up, 'Curse them, they are hounding me! They are insisting on their honour, when it's they who are responsible! They were the ones who gave me to a man I didn't love when I was just sixteen, still only a child. And now that the wastrel has abandoned me, they want me to live alone and unprotected with nobody to love, like some solitary bird! Ah, cruel world!' And with this she seized Yoryis by the hand and tried to drag him to the door. Then with mounting anxiety she added, 'Go, then, go . . . alone, if that's what you want! . . . I've tried this one last time to win your heart. Forgive me. I was consumed by jealousy and caused a scandal. But go, time is running out!'

Yoryis looked at her stunned, and despite himself tears came to his eyes.

'God will forgive you much,' he said, 'because you've a kind heart.' He stood there in silence a moment, considering what to do.

'Leave,' she repeated, pushing him towards the door.

By now they could hear dogs barking.

'They're coming,' cried Vasiliki beginning to panic. 'Leave at once.'

'It's too late!'

'There's still time!' she said opening the door, 'quick, down the hill and back up the other side to the village; stay in hiding at home tonight and tomorrow flee abroad. Don't worry about me, I'm not afraid of them.'

For a moment he stood hesitating in the doorway. But she pushed him out with all her might.

'I'll hide nearby until they leave,' he muttered. 'If they try to harm you I'll reveal myself at once.' And with this he ran helter-skelter for the olive grove.

Meanwhile the barking continued and soon the sound of footsteps and angry cries rang out, the hue and cry increasing by the minute as the party approached the hut.

'Here they come,' said Vasiliki to herself, flinging her headscarf to the ground defiantly, her back against the doorpost, 'this is where I'll make my stand!'

Soon she could make them out. There were about ten men altogether, some holding lanterns, others armed with guns or heavy sticks.

'We've caught them both,' cried her brother Kostas, evidently the leader of the gang, who had seen her silhouette against the light from the door. 'Surround the hut so they don't escape!'

The others hastened to obey him.

'What are you looking for?' asked Vasiliki fiercely.

Three men, Maria's two brothers and one of her own cousins, came up to her.

'Where is Yoryis?' growled one of the brothers in a husky voice.

'Don't talk to her,' her cousin ordered him.

'I don't know,' replied Vasiliki, 'he's not here,' and she stood aside to let them in.

The three young men entered and searched high and low, but not finding anyone came out again.

'And you,' her cousin said to her, 'what are you doing here at this hour?'

'My fate brought me here,' she replied defiantly. 'You may be my kinsmen, but I don't acknowledge you as brothers. As I've said before, you set me up for scandal from the start. Yes all of you, God damn you!'

'What are we going to do with her?' asked Maria's brother.

'Who's going to risk his life and soul for that whore?' shouted Kostas from behind, 'I'll pack her off to town tomorrow and she can practice her profession there.'

'True enough,' agreed two or three others.

'What now?' someone asked.
'Let's go and find him.'
'He'll be hiding among the bushes.'
'Vasiliki will know.'
'Where is he, Vasiliki?'
'Probably at home.'
'Let's go and see!'
'She's not giving anything away!'
'Let's go past his house,' said Kostas, 'and if we don't find him, tomorrow is another day, he won't escape!'
'Yes, let's go,' the rest of them agreed.
And they set off.
'Go with God's curse!' Vasiliki shouted after them, re-entering the hut.

That same evening, while the icon painter and his wife were downstairs eating their supper in gloomy silence, Maria came knocking on their door. Eftymia went and opened it, but when she saw who it was slammed it shut again at once!
'Open up,' cried Maria, 'I must speak to you.'
'Who is it?' asked the painter turning pale.
'It's Maria,' his wife replied, flustered.
'Well, aren't you going to let her in, woman? The way things have turned out, the best thing is for him to marry her!'
The old woman opened the door again and Maria entered, pale and agitated.
'Where's your son?' she asked without pausing to greet them.
'Be patient, daughter, welcome to our home, no one's going to throw you out. Yoryis will be here soon . . .' And as he said this, the painter stepped forward to embrace her.
'They're after him,' Maria cried, evading the old man. 'They are determined to kill him tonight!'
'Woe is us,' the mother wailed, clutching her head with her hands. 'How do you know this?'
'And what about you,' asked the artist with a sigh, looking at her gently, 'aren't you gratified by his misfortune, since he's wronged you? Have you come alone?'

'I pitied you for your bereavement,' she said weeping, 'and then . . . I felt heartsick because I once loved him so very much. But where can he be?'

'We don't know,' they replied in unison and the artist added stoically, raising his eyes toward heaven, 'Whatever is ordained will happen, how can a frail old man like me defend him?'

'Could he be at the hut?' asked Maria, clasping her hands in despair.

'He wasn't there earlier,' replied the old woman anxiously, 'but he might have returned by now.'

'If he's gone there he is doomed,' said the girl dejectedly.

The old woman again started lamenting.

'No need to cry foul before anything's occurred,' the artist told her gloomily. 'There'll be time enough for tears later. Now let us go upstairs. But whatever happens, Maria, whether he lives or dies, you will always be my daughter.'

The women obeyed at once. Taking the blackened lamp from the wall, the old woman made her way upstairs, followed by Maria, the artist bringing up the rear. At the head of the stairs all three paused instinctively before the icon and crossed themselves, privately murmuring a payer. Then the two women wept a little, while the artist brooded in silence.

Suddenly they heard the door, which the old woman had forgotten to bolt, burst open and slam shut, followed by the sound of the bar being hastily drawn across.

'It's Yoryis,' exclaimed the icon painter with the faintest smile.

'The Virgin be praised!' Maria cried, 'they haven't found him.'

'My son!' sobbed the old woman.

Almost immediately Yoryis appeared upstairs. He was pale and out of breath.

'They're after me,' he declared at once without bidding them good evening and sat down on a stool. 'They're here already. I don't know what they'll do!'

'Alas my son,' moaned the old woman, 'how you've poisoned our old age.'

The artist looked at him in alarm, while Maria went and stood beside him.

'They'll soon be at the door,' said Yoryis. 'But what's Maria doing here?'

'She came to warn you, reprobate,' the artist told him in a husky voice. 'You frankly don't deserve such a wife.'

'I don't want him,' declared the young girl resolutely. 'He's far too dissolute. I just didn't want to see him die. I'm going to withdraw to a monastery for ever, since I can't return home a bride.'

The old woman, who had been whimpering with fear and muttering, 'What further shocks await me in old age?' now began to wail without restraint.

Her shrieks quickly caused a stir among the neighbours. Doors began to open and people emerged into the street to find out what had happened at the icon painter's house, as everyone was expecting that Yoryis would be killed that evening. Women appeared at their windows and hung lamps from the shutters, eager to see what was happening below or catch a glimpse of the victim's corpse, should it be borne up from the valley. So that in the middle of the night the peaceful village now became a scene of noise and tumult, every so often a woman could be heard weeping, and steadily the crowd increased.

Everyone was asking what was going on.

Suddenly hurried steps and the harsh cries of angry and determined men were heard. Then the crowd caught sight of the gang heading with their guns and torches for the artist's house, and immediately people realized what was about to happen. For a moment there was silence and everybody shuddered. But by now the armed men were amongst them, jostling the crowd and vociferously threatening and cursing Yoryis. 'The villain is upstairs,' cried Kostas pointing to the house.

'The scoundrel mustn't get away,' shouted one of Maria's brothers.

'Stathis!' 'Nikolas!' 'Petros!' and other names could be heard above the hubbub.

A few people tried to intervene.

But then a cry arose, which many in the crowd picked up and chanted, 'They're right! The dirty rat deserves all he gets!'

And the people, responding to some obscure primordial impulse deep within them, parted and let the armed men through.

'He must die tonight!' one member of the gang roared savagely.

'Yes, yes!' cried several of his clansmen.

The crowd shuddered. The women at the windows started beating their breasts and wailing.

By now they were on the point of breaking down the icon painter's door, storming into the house and finishing their business. But at that very moment Maria appeared at the window in tears and, trembling from head to foot, called out to each of her brothers by name, 'Vasilis, Spyros, Petros!'

'Quiet, lads,' her eldest brother commanded his companions. 'Wait a minute and let's see what we should do. The situation seems to be changing.'

'What d'you mean, changing?' cried Kostas, battering at the door with the butt of his gun. 'We're going to settle things tonight.'

'Vasilis,' Maria again cried from the window.

'You've done the right thing,' Vasilis called out to her, 'and in the nick of time. Your rival's at the hut, so you sit tight. Is Yoryis with you? Have they accepted you?'

'Yes,' she replied, nodding her head vigorously.

'Let's go home, lads,' said Vasilis on hearing this. 'Our sister's getting married. She's in good hands now.'

'What?' Kostas retorted angrily, 'you celebrate a wedding and we bear all the shame?'

'The agreement was that he'd be killed tonight!'

'And if not tonight, tomorrow!'

'Clear off home,' shouted many in the crowd.

'Now they'll fight it out between them,' others muttered.

'Be off, lads, and God speed, ' urged the majority.

'I defy anyone to touch him,' Vasilis now cried menacingly.

The two clans drew apart and confronted one another. Maria's kinsmen outnumbered their opponents.

'Let's get to bed,' said one of them.

'Yes and God speed,' shouted the crowd.

'Our honour is at stake,' protested Kostas.

The artist was watching from the window and listening to everything. And at that very moment he turned towards the icon and, raising his eyes to the sacred image, said, 'It's now, most holy Virgin, now that I need the miracle. No blood must be shed because of him.'

Vasilis meanwhile was angrily replying, 'Your clan has always been dishonourable. Vasiliki's a whore. All five villages know this! Do you intend to kill our bridegroom for a common slut?'

'I shall bear you in procession to the church,' the artist continued, addressing the icon.

Outside, a knife had already flashed and the hubbub was increasing.

'Don't, don't!' cried the crowd in the street and several women at the windows.

Then suddenly the icon painter's door swung open. For a moment there was a lull in the fracas and everybody waited to see what would happen next. Maria's kinsmen were assessing how they might defend the entrance, Vasiliki's how they might take the place by storm. But all eyes were now drawn to the large icon in the doorway, as the light fell upon it from the surrounding windows. The archangel arrayed in white seemed huge, as if he were now barring entry to the painter's house. The icon took up the entire doorway.

Everyone was taken aback. Instinctively the angry kinsmen concealed their knives in the presence of the angel, and at once many in the crowd surged forward to part the quarrelling factions.

'Make way, make way!' shouted several voices. 'The procession of the miracle-working icon is commencing! Be fearful of the Lord!'

By now the icon had passed through the door and, swaying from side to side, was advancing towards the crowd. All the men shuddered, doffed their hats and crossed themselves, and the women at the windows said their prayers.

Complete silence reigned.

Then at a measured pace the archangel was paraded through the village, the people following devoutly as they proceeded to the church, every voice uttering a spontaneous prayer and chanting with mingled gratitude and awe: 'Hail, Mary full of grace!'

1910

WAS IT A SIN?

It was dawn on a cool April morning — Easter Sunday morning. The sun had not yet risen and the bells of the village church were pealing, inviting the faithful to attend the service. People were crowding through the doors, everyone looking happy, radiant and spruce in their best clothes as they filed in, bowed devoutly before the icons, and made their way to their places in the stalls. The women arrived in clusters, their heads covered with white kerchiefs, gold trinkets at their bosoms, looking modest and devout in all their finery, and stood together in a group at the back of the church, as there was no women's gallery.

Everyone was now waiting for the service to begin.

The vestry door opened, there was a shuffling of feet, the priest finished his preliminary rites, shook the censer, gave a little cough, stood in silence before the iconostasis for a moment,* crossed himself and then in a high sonorous voice began the service. Everyone made the sign of the cross.

The celebrant clad in golden robes was elderly, a short thin man with a full white beard and long silvery hair, his forehead wrinkled and his blue eyes faded with the years and frequent fasting. In the village he was universally revered.

With his high-pitched voice steadily becoming stronger, the old man intoned the litany, all of which he knew by heart, and as always the service proceeded solemnly, grandly and devoutly, while the congregation, holding lighted tapers in their crossed hands, listened and responded with piety and ardour, as if the importance of this festival enhanced the merits of their prayers.

But the priest was not at ease.

The first time he stood before the screen door to bless them, he cast his faded eyes over the congregation as if seeking someone, and his heart beat faster as he caught sight of an elderly man in the front row who also seemed distracted, since he was not standing motionless and lost in prayer like the others. 'She must be here too,' the priest said to himself. But he did not have time to locate her among the other women.

Now the euphonious sound of choristers chanting hymns and the smell of incense filled the church, and the faithful responded to the tremulous invocations of the priest with one voice, ardently beseeching the celestial powers for mercy, anxious for their prayers to ascend to the very throne of God, longing to subdue their demons and submit to the will of the Almighty.

The priest read on, now murmuring almost in a whisper, now chanting sonorously, but minute by minute his preoccupation was increasing and he read out the sacred verses dealing with Christ's sacrifice mechanically; other worries filled his mind, other matters overwhelmed his heart as he prayed to the heavenly Father. Was he destined to commit a sin?

Yes, she was here too! He had noticed her as he shook incense over the crowd, half hidden among the other women. The young girl's distress, her fear and agitation were all plainly written on her pretty face. Ah, the poor wretch, it was not her fault either. Her father, the old man standing in the front row but not praying, had insisted she attend. How she had wept the other day during confession, when broken-hearted she had admitted her great sin, her fateful desperate passion for a married man. She herself would never have dared to take communion, but her father had obliged her to, he needed confirmation, he wanted either to be proud of his daughter or to wash their shame away in blood!

What was the poor girl to do? And how perturbed the priest had been as he had listened to her! Why had God let him go on living, only to plunge him into such an impossible predicament in his old age, why did he not have compassion on his flock instead of allowing them to sin, why did he not bind the powers of the Tempter once and for all?

And the service continued. Bearing the sacraments between two candles, he emerged before the sanctuary and stood facing the congregation. No one stirred and complete silence reigned. As he prayed for the people in his high falsetto voice, a shiver ran down every spine and the 'Christ have mercy on us' that came from every lip arose from deep within them, from quaking hearts made humble at that moment by fear of their own weakness. But the old priest did not lower his gaze as normally. With his faded eyes he peered into the depths of the church where the women stood, as if anxious to catch the miscreant's eye and

WAS IT A SIN?

reinforce the instructions he had given her the other day at her confession.

He could not, he had expressly told her, let her take communion. No, he could never consider such a sin. Far better for her not to come to church at Easter, for her to make up some excuse, to say that she was ill. If however she could not get out of it and was obliged to come, she should present herself with all the other women and he would pretend to administer the body and blood of Christ to her. No, he could not let her take communion, the sin was too grave to contemplate.

And the service continued. He had already read the lesson from the Gospels and was now hurriedly chanting the remaining hymns, and all the while his heart was becoming more and more uneasy. Would God wish him to commit this sin, or would He permit bloodshed in the village on account of him, and let people weep and the Tempter rejoice in the abyss? Yes, the priest now feared that his little understanding with the girl might not succeed. He noticed that the closer the moment of communion approached the more restless the father was becoming, perhaps because he wished to see his daughter receive the eucharist with his own eyes, so as to be completely certain.

By now the service was almost at an end. They had recited the creed and the Lord's prayer, the choristers had chanted the introit and the revered old priest now stood in his golden robes before the sanctuary, inviting the faithful to partake. His hands were trembling, as if the silver chalice were too heavy for him. He glanced in her direction and started administering to the communicants, who as always on this momentous festival were numerous.

The first to come forward were the old men, each turning to the congregation and asking for forgiveness; then came the other men and finally the women. She too was among them. Now and then the priest would steal a glance at her. But he also noticed her elderly father getting more and more agitated as he observed her giving way to others, and he could see him watching like a hawk and edging ever closer. Then as in a trance and looking pale as death, she hesitantly came forward and placed her foot on the first step. Her father next to her was watching. Then to his delight he saw the saintly old man, now serene, holding the tongs with the consecrated morsel to her lips, as in his high-pitched voice he uttered the ritual words: 'For the forgiveness of sins and the life everlasting.'

Karousades, 1912

NOTES

These notes correspond to asterisks in the text. The heading for each note consists of the extract from the text to which the note refers, preceded by the page number. Full details of works referred to will be found in the Bibliography.

FACE DOWN

1. Magoulades
A village in the north-west of Corfu Island. This story was based on an actual incident from the Greek Revolutionary period, involving a certain Andonis Vrachnos, known as Koukouliotis, which was orally transmitted by his sons to Theotokis' father, Count Markos, who recorded it in the archives pertaining to the period of the Heptanesian Republic.

2. 'I'll wash away the dishonour you have brought on me, you shameless creature!' Modern anthropologists have pointed out that in contrast to Japan, honour and shame in Mediterranean and Muslim cultures are closely linked to female chastity. Honour killings in Theotokis' day, though illegal and against Christian teaching, were still sanctioned by custom.

NOT DONE YET?

3. The millstone was revolving . . . the press extruded oil
'A perpendicular stone wheel, revolving on a large horizontal stone of a circular form, and slightly hollowed in the centre, is set in motion by a horse, and bruises the olives, which are shovelled in by a peasant. They are then placed in a mat bag, and pressed by means of a clumsy screw, the oil oozing through the bag into a hole cut in the ground.' (Jervis, 259)

3. Over at Ermones
Ermones is due west of Corfu Town on the west coast.

4. Gallows Fork
A legacy of British rule perhaps, when 'gallows could apparently be seen in many public places throughout the Seven Islands.' (Potts, 72)

NOTES

CAIN

7. What do we elect M.P.s for? Our own convenience, of course.
'Manhood suffrage came very early to the uneducated peasants of new Greece [...] To these a vote is, naturally, regarded as something personally useful [...] That their M.P. should procure them a road, or contrive that a sentence passed should not be executed on their cousin the murderer, is the nearest approach one can expect to patriotism.' (Atkinson, 154)

12. Ten fivers
The Greek term *talaro* (derived like 'dollar' from the German *Taler*) was commonly used in Theotokis' time to refer to a silver five-drachma coin.

13. smugglers near the beach at Kalami
Kalami, where Lawrence Durrell and his first wife Nancy resided in the 1930s, is on the north east coast of Corfu, directly across from Albania. In Theotokis' day, high tariffs imposed by Athens made smuggling from Turkish territory a lucrative proposition. His novel *Honour and Cash* (1912), opens dramatically with the heroine hiding a sack of sugar for her prospective son-in-law, a patrician turned smuggler being pursued by the police.

VILLAGE LIFE

17. Petros took the insult very much to heart and was incensed
According to a classic ethnographic study of mountain village life in neighbouring Epirus, in this situation 'the action of the girl's family which is most likely to give grave offence to the man and his kinsmen is not the breaking of the betrothal contract, but unwillingness to enter it at all. Even if the refusal is made through the negotiator, the situation is serious enough [...] In the event of the refusal being made after the brother or father of the man has made a formal request for the girl's hand, the situation is much graver.' (Campbell, 129)

18. Saint Spyridon
The patron saint and protector of Corfu, whose preserved body, kept in the Italianate church named after him, is paraded round the town four times a year: 'on Palm Sunday because on that day in 1630 he relieved the island of the plague; on Easter Saturday because on that day in 1553 the saint saved the island from famine; on 11 August because on that date in 1716 he relieved the island from the siege by Turkish forces; and on the first Sunday of November because in 1673 he intervened once more, again saving Corfu from the plague'. (Leontsini, 64, with items rearranged in calendar, rather than historical order)

NOTES

20. It was a Sunday during Carnival
This period of revelry preceding Lent, broadly corresponding to Shrove-tide, was less important in Greek Orthodox tradition than in Catholic countries, particularly hedonistic Venice, and contemporary accounts suggest that Carnival celebrations on Corfu were comparatively modest.

21. the *syrto*
The *syrto*, from the Greek verb *syro* meaning 'drag', is a line dance of ancient origin described by Lucian in the first century AD, and still popular on the Greek islands. With the *kalamatianos*, which has the same steps danced to a slightly different rhythm, it has followed the Greek diaspora and become one of the two most familiar national Greek dances

24. around Annunciation day
March 25th, traditionally known in English-speaking countries as Lady Day.

26. they had the same godparent at their baptism
People who have the same godparent become spiritual siblings (*kaladelphi*) and cannot marry according to strict Orthodox teaching.

REPUTATION

29. In the cleft between two steep, densely wooded hills [...] villagers of Skaphidaki Historically villages even near the coast were often built high up as a protection against marauding pirates, and in Theotokis' stories the women typically descend from them to graze their sheep.

29. their hollow twisted trunks all gnarled and knotted.
In contrast to the practice on Zante, olive trees on Corfu were not pruned, and consequently though they grew to a great age their yield was unpredictable. Typically the crop was harvested by women gathering the olives from the ground and towards the end of the season beating the trees.

32. *Pretty little basil plant* [...] *I'm the one you're wedding*
Such couplets known as *mandinades* (from the Venetian *matinada*, or afternoon serenade) spread from Crete and were often spontaneously composed and sung at weddings and festivities, where Theotokis, who shared the contemporary interest in folksong, would make a note of them. He uses this same couplet again in 'Illicit Love' (page 75).

35. strawberry trees
The common name for *Arbutus andrachne*, a shrub or small tree native to the Mediterranean with edible red berries that have a strawberry-like flavour. Fruit

is delayed for about five months after pollination, so that fresh flowers appear while the previous year's fruits are ripening.

41. some in narrow trousers, others in wide baggy ones, some with straw hats, others with a fez Traditional and western dress still coexisted, as the contemporary pictorial record shows, and Theotokis used the contrast consistently to make points about character and the changing times.

43. We'll burn the house down!
Communal burning of houses as punishment for certain crimes or in vendettas was common in the Balkans, particularly Albania.

HONOURABLE PEOPLE

p. 45. Ropila
Perhaps a village in the Ropa Valley, west of Corfu Town.

STALAKTI'S WEDDING

54. You Judas!
Apart from its dramatic appropriateness, this curse is a reminder of the local belief that Judas Iscariot found refuge in Corfu, a legend linked to the anti-Semitic Easter ritual of throwing old pots out of windows onto the street in a symbolic stoning.

61. the feast of the Holy Cross
There are several feast days in the Orthodox calendar devoted to the Cross, the one in question falling on September 13th.

63. I can't go to war with my own father
On the Ionian island of Lefkada a man tried for murdering his father with an axe in 1853 confessed that it was 'because the *pater familias* was threatening to disinherit him if he went through with his plans to marry a girl of whom his father disapproved. The son hoped to strike before the father could visit the notary and change his will.' (Gallant, 100)

ILLICIT LOVE

69. a native of Daphnyla.
There is a Daphnyla Bay on the east coast a few miles north of Corfu Town.

69. dressed in western clothes
See the note to page 41.

NOTES

69. How are things going [...] I don't think we've ever seen such bounty The manuscript of 'Illicit Love' suffered water damage while buried for safety during the Second World War. The posthumously published Greek text prints a number of incomplete sentences in the first two pages. In this translation, these have been compressed into continuous text.

71. Marry early or join a monastery
In Greek: *I mikros pandrepsou, i mikros kaloyerepsou*. The saying may be related to the Orthodox custom, dating back to Byzantine times, whereby a man wishing to become a priest must marry before being ordained or remain celibate thereafter.

72. an engagement party
The Greek Orthodox marriage service is in two parts, traditionally held two or three months apart: the Office of Betrothal, in which the exchange of rings occurs, and the Office of Crowning which completes the sacrament and involves the exchange of wreaths.

72. one for each of the bride's and groom's new relatives
The Greek kinship term *sympetheros* means relative by marriage, as distinct from blood relative.

72. *tsarouchia*
Rustic pointed leather Turkish slippers.

75. *mandinada*
Singular of *mandinades* (see the note to page 32).

76. looked back for one last glimpse of the beloved home
The technically 'partilocal' nature of the culture, in which upon marriage the woman moved into the household of her husband's family, and the attendant tensions between bride and mother-in-law, is most explicit in this story but reflected or implicit in a number of the others.

76. On her head she wore a spotless white silk headscarf [...] many-coloured ribbons Still part of life in 1900, Corfu's very varied folk costumes were marks of regional or village identity, historically reflective both of the island's ethnic and cultural mix and of the clannishness and xenophobia of isolated rural communities. High elaborate *bolias*, somewhat different from this one, were worn for instance by Gastouri women: 'On the head a wonderful erection of hair is worked over a double series of cushions, to which it is bound with red ribbons. A fine muslin and lace-edged kerchief is turned back from the crown, and sometimes dotted with tinsel ornaments and coloured flowers', giving these village belles a 'Plantagenet-like' appearance (Atkinson, 87).

NOTES

77. Standing in his pew
Technically the term 'pew' is misleading, since in a Greek Orthodox church the stalls usually run round the walls. The bulk of the congregation attending the service stands in the nave facing the icon-bearing screen dividing them from the sanctuary.

79. the *syrto*
See the note to page 21.

80. *fourlana*
Popular on Corfu, the *fourlana* (also known as the *friulana*) is a lively and sensual Italian folk dance, named after Friuli in the Venetian Republic, and originally a courtship dance performed by a couple.

95. May you be safe from the evil eye
The evil eye was associated with envy and the devil, and someone possessed of it could inflict all manner of ills upon his or her victim, who might seek protection through a wide range of phylacteries and charms.

96. neither woman had much formal education
The Greek *agrammatos* can mean illiterate, or simply uneducated, which seems the better option here, as Diamando has just been urging Chrysavyi to write to Yoryis, and reading could be considered the more onerous task. But the whole passage is fairly loosely written and the inconsistency may have been a slip on Theotokis' part, which he might have rectified had he been able to proofread this posthumously published story.

104. the baby has not yet turned inside the womb
Though not medically trained, Theotokis put his scientific studies in Paris to practical use among his retainers, assisting them and their livestock with basic health and hygiene issues.

TWO LOVES

109. old patched baggy trousers
'The art of patching is much developed. I have seen [...] jackets so intricately and variously patched that none might say whether original garment were there at all, and the full blue cotton skirts of everyday wear are generally varied in gentle degrees of faded patch.' (Atkinson, 90)

110. at least two centuries [...] driven out of Epirus by the Turks
This would have been around 1716, when the Ottoman expansion northward through the Balkans was halted outside Vienna by Prince Eugene, and Corfu was successfully defended by the mercenary Marshall Schulenburg.

NOTES

113. her icon, which will perform miracles for Christian folk
Miracle-working powers were attributed to a painting of the Virgin in a church in the northern port of Kassiopi, less than twenty miles from the Theotokis country residence at Karousades.

114. unlike those icons peddled in town by the accursed Jews
Anti-Semitism, which grew with the commercial success of the Jews in Corfu, was satirized more at length by Theotokis in his novel *Slaves in their Chains*. In the Second World War the Corfiot authorities cooperated in the deportation of the Jews, whereas those of Zakynthos (Zante) refused to do so.

114. from Sidari to Alefki. Sidari is a village on the northwest coast of Corfu; Alefki is probably a contraction of Ano Lefkimmi, a town near its southernmost tip.

116. Sixty lousy fivers
See the note to page 12.

WAS IT A SIN?

143. stood in silence before the iconostasis for a moment
The *Iconostasis*, or icon-bearing screen, like the rood-screen in western churches, separates the congregation from the sanctuary and altar table and usually has three doors, leading to the vestry (on the left), the sanctuary, and a chapel where the sacred texts are kept.

BIBLIOGRAPHY

Works referred to in the Introduction and Notes

Atkinson, Sophie, *An artist in Corfu*. Boston: Este / London: Herbert and Daniel, 1911; reprint London: Forgotten Books, 2015.
Campbell, J. K., *Honour, family and patronage: a study of institutions and moral values in a Greek mountain community*. Oxford: Clarendon, 1964.
Dicks, Brian, *Corfu*. London: David & Charles, 1977.
Gallant, Thomas W., *Modern Greece*. London: Hodder Arnold, 2001.
Herrin, Judith, *Byzantium: the surprising life of a medieval empire*. London: Penguin 2007.
Jenkins, Romilly, *Dionysius Solomós*. Athens: Denise Harvey, 1981; 1st edition Cambridge: Cambridge University Press, 1940.
Jervis, Henry Jervis White, *History of the Island of Corfu and of the Republic of the Ionian Islands*. Amsterdam: B. R. Grüner, 1970 (reprint); 1st edition 1852.
Leontsini, Maria, 'The Ionian Islands during the Byzantine period: an overview of their history and monuments', in Anthony Hirst and Patrick Sammon (eds), *The Ionian Islands: aspects of their history and culture*, 45–82. Newcastle upon Tyne: Cambridge Scholars Publishing, 2014.
Potts, Jim, *The Ionian Islands and Epirus: A Cultural History*. Oxford: Signal Books, 2010.
Young, Martin, *Corfu and the other Ionian Islands*. London: Jonathan Cape, 1977.
Δάλλας, Γιάννης (Yannis Dallas), Κωνσταντίνος Θεοτόκης: κριτική σπουδή μιας πεζογραφικής πορείας (*Konstantinos Theotokis: a critical study of his career as a prose writer*). Athens: Ekdoseis Sokoli, 2001.
Θεοτόκης, Σπυρίδων Μ. (Spyridon M. Theotokis), Τα νεανικά χρόνια του Κωνσταντίνου Θεοτόκη: βιογραφία (*The early years of Konstantinos Theotokis: a biography*), ed. Tasos Korphis. Athens: Prosperos, 1983.
Χουρμούζιος, Αιμίλιος (Emilios Chourmouzios), Κωνσταντίνος Θεοτόκης: ο εισηγητής του κοινωνιστικού μυθιστορήματος στην Ελλάδα (*Konstantinos Theotokis: the founder of the social novel in Greece*). Athens: Ekdoseis ton Philon, 1979.

Further reading

Beaton, Roderick, *An Introduction to modern Greek literature*. Oxford: Clarendon Press, 1994; 2nd edition 1999.
Crawley, Roger, *City of Fortune: how Venice won and lost a naval empire*. London: Faber & Faber, 2011.

Dakin, Douglas, The *unification of Greece 1770-1923*. London: Ernest Benn, 1972.
Durrell, Gerald, *The Corfu Trilogy*. London: Penguin, 2006. Includes *My family and other animals* (1956), *Birds, beasts and relatives* (1969), and *The Garden of the Gods* (1979).
Durrell, Lawrence, *Prospero's Cell: a guide to the landscape and manners of the island of Corcyra*. London: Faber & Faber, 2000; 1st edition 1945.
Flamburiari, Spiro L., *Corfu: the garden isle*. London: John Murray, 1994.
Fleming, K. E., *The Muslim Bonaparte: diplomacy and orientalism in Ali Pasha's Greece*. Princeton: Princeton University Press, 1999.
Gilmore, David D., *Honor and shame and the unity of the Mediterranean*. Arlington, VA: American Anthropological Association, 1987.
Holland, Robert *Blue-water empire: the British in the Mediterranean since 1800*. London: Penguin, 2013.
Karkavitsas, Andreas, *The beggar*, tr. W. F. Wyatt. New York: Caratzas, 1982.
Lear, Edward, *The Corfu years*, ed. Philip Sherrard. Athens: Denise Harvey, 1988.
Mackridge, Peter, *Language and national identity in Greece 1776–1976*. Oxford: Oxford University Press, 2009.
Papadiamantis, Alexandros, *Tales from a Greek island*, tr. Elizabeth Constantinides. Baltimore, MD: The Johns Hopkins University Press, 1987.
Peristiany, J. G. (ed.), *Honour and shame: the values of Mediterranean society*. Chicago: University of Chicago Press, 1966.
Pratt, Michael, *Britain's Greek empire*. London: Rex Collings, 1978.
St Clair, William, *That Greece might still be free: the Philhellenes in the War of Independence*. London: Oxford University Press, 1972.
Theotokis, Konstantinos, *Slaves in their chains*, tr. J. M. Q. Davies. London: Angel Classics, 2014.
———, *The life and death of Hangman Thomas*, tr. J. M. Q. Davies. London: Colenso Books, 2016.
Verga, Giovanni, *Life in the country*, tr. J.G.Nichols. London: Hesperus, 2003.
Vizyenos, Georgios, *My mother's sin and other stories*, tr. William F. Wyatt, Jr. Hanover, NH: University Press of New England, 1988.
Ware, Timothy, *The Orthodox Church: an introduction to Eastern Christianity*. London: Penguin, 2015; 1st edition 1963.

www.ingramcontent.com/pod-product-compliance
Ingram Content Group UK Ltd.
Pitfield, Milton Keynes, MK11 3LW, UK
UKHW042034071125
464835UK00001B/43